The Waw

Also by Jacqueline Gay Walley

"Isn't that what you are running from? The way you stay separate?...I was good at going." In *The Waw*, a wonderful new novel by Gay Walley, a woman makes her own mystery in an English village completely unlike her life in New York. Skene just walks into her life, and Sir Leo, her wry, hundred-year-old tennis partner unpacks romance for her. So knowing with dialogue between men and women, Walley, also a playwright, is a master of erotic tension.

—Terese Svoboda, *Roxy and Coco* and *The Long Swim*

At the center of *The Waw*—an unhurried, psychologically acute novel—is a mature woman's quest for a life determined by her inner compass. On the strength of a vision, the central character, the first-person narrator, "a polite storm of a woman," a writer with a restless nomadic past, leaves New York City and an established relationship for a small, seemingly unchanging British island. Through the course of the book, the narrator examines her past and the world she finds herself in with equal care, coming to trust herself in the process. *The Waw* is a lovely meditation on the challenges and rewards of being true to oneself, no matter the difficulties of our contemporary world.

—Carol Moldaw, *The Widening*

Open this book and let it take you on a nomadic journey: to the oasis of language; to the wandering of stories, yours and others; to the loudness of silence, and the silencing of those with ideas we do not agree with; and to find what it is we are searching for.

—Jeff Talarigo, *In the Cemetery of the Orange Trees*

To read *The Waw* is to slip into a quiet life by the sea where strangers become friends and community heals what ails. Reminiscent of *Under the Tuscan Sun*, this transportive novel is for those who have imagined their lives unspooling someplace new.

—Sari Fordham, *Wait for God to Notice*

The Waw

Jacqueline Gay Walley

Etruscan Press

Etruscan Press
Wilkes University
84 West South Street
Wilkes-Barre, PA 18766
(570) 408-4546

 Wilkes University

www.etruscanpress.org

Published 2024 by Etruscan Press
Printed in the United States of America
Cover design by Jess Morandi
Interior design and typesetting by Aaron Petrovich
The text of this book is set in Miller Text.

First Edition

17 18 19 20 5 4 3 2 1

Library of Congress Cataloguing-in-Publication Data

Names: Walley, Gay, 1951- author.
Title: The Waw / Jacqueline Gay Walley.
Description: First edition. | Wilkes-Barre, PA : Etruscan Press, 2024. |
    Summary: "Dostoyevsky said, Beauty saves, and, in THE WAW, an
    individualistic, creative woman of a certain age follows a vision that
    calls her to a place of great beauty by the sea in England. There she
    encounters remarkable people of strength. The beauty of the place and
    people, in essence, transform her"-- Provided by publisher.
Identifiers: LCCN 2023038973 | ISBN 9798985882490 (paperback acid-free
    paper) | ISBN 9798988198543 (ebook)
Subjects: LCGFT: Novels.
Classification: LCC PS3573.A4355 W39 2024 | DDC 813/.54--dc23/eng/20230828
LC record available at https://lccn.loc.gov/2023038973

Please turn to the back of this book for a list of the sustaining funders of Etruscan Press.

This book is dedicated to all those who believe there is always something good out there for them, and it just takes saying, "Yes."

Thank you to Terese Svoboda, Katherine Arnoldi and Roberta Allen for listening to this as I sailed along.

Chapter One

There are people who do not settle in one place, but are like the nomadic tribes of the desert, who long for the Waw, the ultimate oasis, where they will finally be home. Until then, they are on the move, taking sustenance from one little oasis to another, following the birdsongs of the desert for messages, and they know, in their souls, the Waw does not really exist, but they hold knowledge of it in their hearts, like a true love one does not ever let go of.

I found myself that late afternoon on a type of cliff, over the sea, under a British or French or Scottish grey sky, looking at a small town with steeples and small stone houses, close together, maybe even a bit like arriving in French Canada on a ship, now that I think about it, Montreal where I grew up and did arrive on a ship but at one year old, because I come from nomads myself who searched for their oasis in the new land, and also never found Waw, but they did live interesting nomadic lives from which they never settled. They danced and they loved, and they found intermittent wells and they kept on moving their whole lives, my British father dying in San Diego, and my Austrian mother returning at the end of her life to London, where she had run to from Palestine where she had run to from Europe, and now back to London in her old age, my current age, to a man she loved her whole life. He had been married and she had accepted this love as an oasis, perfect for a nomadic soul, perhaps, but his wife unexpectedly died, and he then came to get my mother to settle with him. Maybe she did find her Waw then, although she was losing her mind on this second trip of her life to London. The heat of her travels and in not ever being settled, and the endlessness of it, perhaps even the memories of what happened to her family in Europe, having burned her in some way.

I stood there recognizing this town by the sea I was looking at but did not know from where or when it had lodged inside me, but it was my Waw. I had somehow found it. The sea was dark beneath the rocks I stood on and I looked to one side of me and for some reason imagined the sight of dead bodies in fishing gear floating next to me. It was strange, of course, but somehow I knew it had something to do with the turning of life. In my own nomadic travels, the desert for me has always been the sea, and the sea does harbor fishermen, fishers of souls, as the Bible calls it, so I was not frightened at the image because the vision passed so quickly, which told me that I was not ready to join them.

To my other side stood a tall slender man, a new friend I had made with not many words, but who looked over, too, at the town, but steadily, and I deemed he must live there. We beheld our site and took in all it was telling us, and shared without words that we understood that this was a place where depth could live. As I say, it may have been his home, but I did not want to ask such a thing because these are not topics for conversation. But standing next to him, for me, was also home because I think anyone who knew this place, never mind lived in it, and I think he did, knew something of meaning, something of meaning that was not to be found in my other life, on the internet, on emails demanding I respond to endless questionnaires, which I never do, and the constant chatter of exterior matters. I would not say that my other life is the tending of camels, but I would say it is the preoccupation with tending.

I stood there overlooking this place that was quiet but happy, it seemed, as the clouds broke a bit and a sliver of sunlight hit one of the aluminum-covered steeples and it seemed it was beckoning me. It's all right, the light seemed to indicate, cross over and let's, as William Carlos Williams once wrote, begin to begin again.

Chapter Two

But before that happened, I had to address my responsibilities, or so, at first, I thought. I had a New York apartment full to the brim. Windowsills grown chipped and old. The ringing of the clock tower nearby no longer of any moment. Books, endless books surrounding me, did I do nothing but read, and yet I know I didn't. But perhaps there was always a book in my hand; I was told even when I was having my teeth cleaned, I read. A *New York Times* reporter I'd known who wrote about publishing dedicated his farewell column to a woman who always carried a book in her hand. I knew he was writing of me, and I knew he found some Waw for him in that. He did not use the word Waw, of course. But he knew it was how I traveled, or that it was my oasis. As were the sea swells in music. Those companions had given me so much interaction and hope and knowledge, but somehow no longer what my soul craved with a driven fixity anymore.

Of course, we all know movement abets pain, but what was this pain? The pain of stasis or the pain of needing the refreshment of undiscovered sights and undiscovered souls, or more likely undiscovered parts of myself. I sat alone in my apartment when I returned from that town by the water. It was odd that I was carrying on so to go somewhere where I would perhaps be even more alone. But going has its reasons, I told myself. I even knew I would miss terribly what it is I have here. That is the nature of leaving.

But still.

I had become a stranger where I lived. I was no longer here abundantly, fruitfully.

Here, all was tenuous. I had a friendly, tolerant boyfriend, but it was not a love affair that insists on itself, one where to look at that person both to be home and to travel. I tended this love, and that tending brought some sweet and even results, but our mutual guardedness, which often manifested as respect, did not break us into the new. It only required that we be pleasant at all times. An agreement that if I am pleasant, he is pleasant.

A betrayal of myself.

I had friends in unhappy marriages, in beginning relationships, unable to be in relationship, and all of it fingered so obsessively. Everyone had built their little houses, their towns in themselves.

Without my having any say in it, I could no longer speak of these things, they had moved away from me.

And my own work, my own work had grown tired. It had been too long of listening to everyone want proof of themselves. Those loud and teeming desires for identity that I could not respond to anymore. I had disappeared in their immensity.

And perhaps I had tired of stories.

I decided to find someone who wanted to begin as the me I was shedding and move that person into my life. I would find someone to be the me who fit into this life, let her masquerade as me, and I—I would slip away, when I was not looking.

Chapter Three

"**I** am leaving for a bit."

"Why?" my boyfriend asked, not believing me for an instant. The sun was streaming in through his penthouse windows. He has a mosaic dining room table, a pasha he is, a man who surrounds himself in color. I was in love with him at the beginning, maybe still was. But we seemed to have tended our love within too tight limits. Limited time together. Limited commitment. Limited risk. In those limits, I had much of myself. True, I could be creative by myself, and I was, I always was. But contiguously, slowly, like a continual sawing down, my imagination of love and desire had to atrophy to fit our proscribed limits. It was dangerous. Imagination needs the unexpected, or a push from without, a call to be more than you were before. It needs, in love, someone saying "Come with me" to somewhere internal or external you are a bit resistant to go to, but when you do go, you can't imagine how you were so stupid to be resistant.

"I've been in the same place a long time," I explained. "I've done the same things. We do the same things."

"But that is good," he said, putting cinnamon on his fruit salad, something that he had heard is good for one's health. "Wait a few months and we can go to Florida."

"I mean I want to move somewhere new," I said.

He looked at me as if I was a bit off.

"Where?" He sliced a piece of cheese for me. I took it.

"It's on the coast of England."

"It rains a lot. You'll hate that."

"It'll be new to me," I said.

"What about your tennis?" he asked, as if New York is the only place that has courts. And even if that town has no courts, was this worthy of consideration? I wasn't looking to entertain myself.

"I am not going professional so what has that got to do with anything?" I asked.

"But you are getting better," he said. Why do men like to talk about these ridiculous things, I thought.

"I'm getting a bit better," I agreed, although I was not sure, "but there are other things in life . . ."

"You're getting a bit old to move about," he now spoke more sonorously. The lecture was about to come. He had placed the napkin on his lap.

I responded, "Diogenes, I think, said that it is at the end of the race, one breaks into a burst of speed. I am not too old to move about."

"Well why are you abandoning me?" This said as a parody of what women have said to him. Or maybe a joke I have made when he walked me halfway home in the morning.

Should I tell him the truth or be pleasant? This was my moment. I have found that the truth when spoken with him just drops in the air as if never said. Or at least he pretends so. Might as well try.

"You believe our success has been in our keeping a distance and, finally, I agree with you. But distance is not the way of love. It is the way of safety, politeness, equitability, friendship."

"At our age one has mostly friendship."

I watched him put Chinese monk fruit as some kind of sugar into his tea. He takes care of his health as if it is the most delicate and intricate of instruments. He is a careful man.

"The heart," I said, "doesn't age."

Fortunately, he didn't go into a trope about heart attacks. Instead, he pursed his lips, his eyes slightly smiling, as if he was making plans for himself. He dipped into his scrambled eggs, as if I had said nothing unusual. He seemed unmoved.

And with this, I knew he had already left me.

Chapter Four

As I prepared to leave, I got a message from the daughter of a famous writer I had known in my twenties. I had lived underneath him for quite a long time in an apartment by the sea and he and I stayed loosely in touch till he died many years ago. She found some correspondence from him to me and wanted me to write a remembrance of him for his society's newsletter. I agreed, out of deference to my youth by making the feelings of that time come alive. She also sent me a photo of him and me, and I could hardly believe I was that person sitting outside on a balcony; mine, I realized, because the vase with the yellow roses was my own. There was fruit and cheese on the table next to me and we were drinking wine. Or at least I was. I was not smiling at him in the photo, I was just looking at him, perhaps listening. I could not read my expression.

Perhaps no one was meant to read my expression in those days. I did not really know who I was.

In the night, instead of my mind preparing to leave for my move to the town with that steeple, I pieced together my twenties and this time of knowing the writer, since I would be writing about him. The two-family house he and I lived in was owned by a sweet, kind minister who gave me, and probably him, an unusually low rent. The writer was on the top floor, I on the bottom. My own place was lovely, with windows over the sea, a small garden where I read many books, not the ones in my apartment now, for I always sold all my books whenever I moved. At night I was a cocktail waitress in a restaurant shaped like a painter's palette on the harbor, and before it opened for the summer, I was a counter waitress at the Cape Ann Diner on Main Street, the only street in this ocean town, working the very early mornings that were dark as I arrived to serve breakfast to the fishermen before they went out on their boats.

I got about on a bicycle. When I looked back on these facts in the night, getting ready to write this piece for the writer's society, I was struck that that grey cove that I looked out over when I lived there was disturbingly similar, at least in feel, to where I was being called to again. The grey cove, the fishermen. In those days, the fishermen were alive, as was I, very much so.

I was young and many men were after me, but that is the province of the young.

I had a piano that I moved in, the piano tuner leaving a note on it, WITH DREAMS COME RESPONSIBILITIES, which I believed Yeats said but I was to learn later was from Delmore Schwartz, a piano that I sold to pay damages when I got into a car crash. I had bought a watercolor seascape I loved by Anthony Thieme that I sold when I got into some other financial mishap.

I spent one winter there, with those heavy, off-white skies that matched the snow-covered cove, and I loved the solitude and beauty and soon I fell in love and, not that soon, because a solitary person can be a contrary person in love, but eventually he and I married. We both moved to the city but then he wanted to return and settle in the sea town we had met each other in, and he did so. I moved on, to an even bigger city. That bigger city felt like ocean waves I wanted to ride on.

But now here my heart wanted to travel again, to another place like where I had been with my ex-husband, and that tall man who stood by me looking at the British village was similar to my ex-husband in build and aspect. My ex, when we were married, would stand by me as we looked out at the fishing trawlers, and he would say, "See those wings on the boat?"

I nodded.

"Those are called birds." And I never loved him so much for saying that.

Once my ex-husband and I got together, we began following the sea everywhere, Canada, England, and back, sitting together on beaches looking out, as if we were egrets. It was sweet and difficult and what it is meant to be.

And our love only ended when I, like the man I am with now, began talking limits. It was me, me who said I have to pull up, go back with people who are crossing, eternally crossing their destinies. I am not meant for a house, garden, a car, roots. There is something out there, I said. I have to go to it.

"The nomads cross," he replied, "to get somewhere. To get somewhere and stay."

"No, no," I said, "the real ones who cross are not going to a destination. They are crossing back and forth as who they are." Within the desert and themselves.

My husband, bless him, ran his hands through his hair in despair. He had been told by many I was that type, don't marry her, even if she is the love of your life, and you are hers, don't marry her, she is not used to a home life. She's been raised as a nomad.

But she married me, he would tell himself. She wants to stay, in spite of herself.

"I do love you," I said, "so much. But I am not suited to what you want. Materiel, as you call it. It is not who I am. I have no choice."

To my husband's and my great sadness, this turned out to be true.

* * *

As I lay in bed remembering all this, I could see I had been after the Waw a long time and maybe even found it for a while. This woman calling me to write about her writer father must be one of the birds sending messages to me that I had done this before, many times. Gone to a sea town, away from a sea town to the city, which I thought was a sea, away again. It seemed nowhere caught me, not even the Waw.

Chapter Five

I left and took little. Just a suitcase. It was a wonderful feeling to travel so light. But I was not yet leaving for the Waw. My boyfriend and I were on our way to visit my boyfriend's son and his wife for Christmas. The young couple have a small house in Washington, the sort of poster of a small, charming house, with paintings and a sophisticated music set-up, warm rugs and big couches. The son is a five-star chef who prepares for us wines and shucked oysters and cooked halibut on the grill, and we watch iconic movies together that they, being young, have never seen.

As my boyfriend and I drove down together, I tried once again to explain why I needed to leave. That our love had some anemia to it, and that bothered me.

He said, "We do have a life together. A good one. When I made a real home with other women, it didn't work. When I was in love, I made bad choices. I love you but am not in love with you. This is better."

"But what does your failure with other women have to do with me?"

"It just does."

As we passed Baltimore and its ships in a working harbor, I couldn't help but smart at the whole idea that he was not in love with me. I felt like it meant I was not magical enough to evoke such passion, even though he was right that it was his and my relationship that had lasted.

This was all familiar to me. This scratching at reasons to leave, I had done it with my ex, every man, in fact. It was, in short, an old pattern of mine. I despised this about myself.

But I also reflected, as I looked out the window of the car in silence, on how people suddenly after their companionable lover leaves, often find someone they marry two weeks later, with whom, in other words, they fall in love. That could happen to him. That could happen to me. I thought about how this boyfriend and I do get along, extremely well, with a few disappointments on both sides, but overall we are extremely nice to each other. But we don't move heaven and earth and furniture to be together. We don't say we can't live without each other. We don't feel we would die without the other.

But maybe that is age. When you get older, you realize that even the ten thousand small cuts of life are mitigated by the twenty thousand pleasures.

I thought maybe it was my pride that hurt because he did not want to marry me or live with me, yet, in truth, I've never rushed toward marriage myself so why was it I wanted someone to want to marry me?

To make matters worse, as his son and son's wife exchanged Christmas gifts with us, my boyfriend gave me $3000 for my tennis lessons. It was shockingly generous. I do love tennis and seem intent on becoming good at it. How does one leave someone so kind?

I was thoroughly confused.

Maybe I was in my Waw and didn't know it. I certainly was capable of that kind of blindness.

I was going to go off and leave this for an imaginary town? An imaginary life?

Is this wise?

Is it intelligent to hurt a man who has brought me into his family's home and bought me thousands of dollars of tennis lessons? He is obviously being loving to me. He and I like many of the same things, dinner by the fire, humor. There must be another way to get to that town with the steeple that I had been called to for no seeming reason, without causing pain to this man whom I have tenderly loved for twelve years.

Perhaps I could convince him to go with me and he would transform into that man who had stood beside me, that man who seemed to somehow pull my whole soul into his without even saying a word.

Maybe that should be the plan. I'll get my boyfriend to go with me.

Chapter Six

The next day I spoke to my brothers because it was Christmas. One is in Holland, he had moved there, after having lived in maybe twenty other places, and traveled repeatedly round the world. My other brother, in England, also is an inveterate traveler and, in fact, he was away in Cornwall when I called him.

But I think a Waw is where you go to stay. It is the ultimate destination. There is no place better, except perhaps movement.

But it was interesting to me that these brothers move around so. Our conversations were about where they were traveling.

What are we all searching for?

My boyfriend's family are located. They are putting stakes in the ground, thick, deep ones. Houses. Babies. Family dinners and games and talk of food. It cannot be thick enough.

My boyfriend is like me in many ways in that he is not trying to put those kind of roots down but, on the other hand, he is not from nomads.

My brothers and I were children of broken connections, where people were forced to get on the road, due to war or poverty or believing in romance and imagination so much that they followed another romance and its imagination onto another. Flight.

I have no reason now to get away, but I still want to. Has running become part of my DNA because of my background, without my intention? We adapt to circumstances, we humans, and then that becomes part of us.

That must be it.

But I am assailed with feelings of love for my boyfriend, even while being well aware of how he does not insist on a life with me, does not create with me, does not sit down and think how wonderful to see the sun go down together, or sit by the sea together, or sit through a rainstorm together. Instead, he sits through all these alone with his possessions, which seem to give him comfort.

He and his relatives, over Christmas, talk about the advantages of neighbors, their experiences growing up. I don't remember cousins coming over, and aunts and uncles, like they do, but instead I remember ice skating, moving with gusto on the ice, round and round a rink as if loneliness were chasing me. I had a bicycle that I rode, up and down, up and down, to feel free. Later I walked city streets, in high boots, forward, toward I did not know what.

Then there was, when I got a bit older, alcohol for immediate trips when needed.

Chatter, chatter, I hear them in the living room. My boyfriend so happy, reminiscing raising his son. His daughter-in-law excited, about to have a child. They sit and talk about dangerous things that could happen.

These dangerous things sound perfectly safe to me.

Parents wanting to be protective. Mine didn't believe in that. Life had not been protective of them. Why should it be for anyone else?

It occurred to me I might never be able to get away from here at all. My stasis more pronounced than my desire for the other. If something here was burning wrong, it would be easy. But, in truth, I like my walk-through home here. I like my rejecting boyfriend. Nothing is gnawing at me.

I read my mail of newsy letters, people getting their MFAs, even if they are in their seventies. Their letters full of Maugham and Ford Madox Ford. This time travel seemed to be working for them.

But it didn't seem right for me.

I guessed it would be like love, the desire to act would sneak up on me. It would just be clear. Go forward now.

What was holding me here though? Habit.

Listening to *The Carnival of the Animals*, as if it were an old friend.

I must not forget that happiness is out there too, somewhere I do not know.

I must not let fear and familiarity override me.

I must remember comfortability is a palliative, resting point, between experiencing more.

I must remember that adventure teaches.

Chapter Seven

I strengthened my resolve to go. Otherwise, I would be plagued with regret. Time is not infinite, I reminded myself.

Meanwhile, I was having a drink with an old friend. I knew him when we were both young and single, then he married a woman who turned into a gay minister, then he was single again, then he ecstatically married his first love, whom he had worked with as a busboy in Block Island, who was now middle-aged, like him. She got a terminal illness the first year of their marriage. After that, he ended up staying single, living an almost isolated life, and became a thriller writer.

He used to refer to himself as a sultan at our fulsome dinners where we would talk about everything, after which he would insist we go to a Broadway musical since he said they were anti-depressants.

He was a bit philosophical and psychological when he spoke, and I enjoyed this. "This Waw business of yours is a state of mind."

Just like a man, I thought. To have to nail it down. "Of course it is," I said. "Even for the nomads."

"It doesn't exist, it's an illusion," he confirmed, as if I needed confirmation. It was the very thing I didn't want.

"You had the experience of the Waw," he said, "when you were married, you know. You two lived a rather free-wheeling, idyllic, passionate lifestyle. I sort of admire that you want to find it again."

We were in my apartment, and as I listened, I glanced around at all my books. My ex-husband had built the bookcases. I wanted to throw them all out. They had walled me in.

My friend and I changed the subject and began talking about money and the lack of it from one's artistic work, and the need for money to promote the very work that doesn't make money.

Writers talk about this kind of thing, not about how Tolstoy opened the vein. I couldn't, for the life of me, understand the disconnect of money and art.

"I did my part," I said. "I wrote the work. Why should I need to find money for it too?"

"Money is such an interesting question," he replied.

"I don't know. Is it? Not as interesting as it thinks it is."

He smiled, then looked at me, eyes narrowed, as if I was indeed going somewhere but not where I thought. I wouldn't disagree with that, although it was a bit unsettling.

"The thing is I don't have many years left, " I said.

"What do you mean?" he asked.

"I don't mean I am ill. I mean I just don't have this wide expanse before me. Life is tender now, to be treated magisterially." I felt like I was in a YA novel, saying that.

He let me get away with it. "Strange to see you be practical or down to earth at this late date."

"I didn't say practical. Do you think picking up and changing my life is the least bit practical?" I asked.

"No."

"The conundrum is that, if I don't do it, it's just as impractical because I am ignoring my fate."

"Who was it that said your fate involves going off somewhere where you know no one except a view and have imagined dead fishermen?"

I laughed.

"Don't you think you're a bit old to move about like this?" he continued. I'd heard that from Kurt, my boyfriend, too.

"Freud," I replied, "said there is no time in the mind. I know you hate him."

"Okay, I'll give him that," my friend replied. He stared at the fire. "So when do you think you'll go?"

"I am working on it. I have to sort of adjust somehow to hurting people I have come to love by leaving. Friends. Kurt. All of that. It bothers me."

"I can see that," he said, "but you've been after some internal vision nobody understood all your life. They won't be surprised, believe me. I've watched you push away thousands of things, things that can get in the way, like fame, or marriage, or jealousy or ownership—you've said no in every case. You went along with your knapsack, riding along in the desert, stopping, as you call it, at oases, but never staying once you got the lay of the land, and out you went again in the blinding sun, like a bloody fool, only to find another oasis, or somehow make contact with some other type like yourself who was also in passing but you recognized each other and gave each other some comfort, but not too much because you both had to be on your way. But somehow someone always showed up when there were severe storms, opened their tent to you, which is pretty damn lovely—"

I smiled, enjoying his little performance.

"But even more lovely is that they let you leave once they'd come to love you," he said. "Did you ever think how lovely that was of them?"

He sounded a bit angry.

"I did," I replied. Where was he going with this?

"Did you really?" he asked.

"Well, if you must know, you know, when you leave people, you have to sort of build a case for yourself of why you are doing it. That requires certain exaggerations I suppose, which is, perhaps, not so admirable, and what's worse not even so truthful, but"—I looked plaintively at him—"it's what you have to do."

"To slough off the old skin?" he asked, sipping his negroni.

I shrugged my shoulders. I was already depressed just thinking about it.

"I would much prefer to be able to change," I explained, "in some elegant ice dancer's quick triple axel or something but I lack, I guess, that grace."

He flashed eyes at me and then looked back down. He obviously felt somewhat vindicated by that very thin apology, although I wasn't sure what I was apologizing for.

"We've always been friends, so have I hurt you?" I asked quickly.

"Friends, my dear, have feelings too."

That shut me up. I didn't even want to bother saying the usual "I did the best I can" speech.

I sipped on my vodka and tonic.

"I'm not angry," he said. "It's not easy to slip away. I know that," he added.

I said nothing.

Then I said, "You're right."

Chapter Eight

I woke up, shoulder hurting, sun coming in through the windows, and realized there is nothing wrong with me for wanting to go somewhere new. A friend wrote me of a writer in Cornwall who now wants to move to Ireland for some peace and quiet. Why am I acting like I want to invent the hydrogen bomb?

But what knowledge do we think we garner from a nomadic lifestyle? Are we preparing for the final moving on? Like the fishermen? Or do we want to move to be new again in a new place?

The newsletter where I wrote the remembrance of the writer whom I lived underneath in my twenties sent the proof, and included a photo of the place where we were living. As I suspected, it looked exactly like the Waw. Had I already been to the Waw, as my friend last night suggested, and now I want to return? A sort of recherche of les temps perdu?

Anyway, I couldn't go back to that place. I have an ex-husband living there with a wife and I do not want to run into them all the time, even though I love both of them, but I would always feel I was the ghost of the past haunting. I also have an ex-lover there, who is married, and I do not want to run into him either and end up making banal jokes like "How's marriage?" "Oh, you know," he would say, "you become like brother and sister," and he'd laugh, and I'd laugh and I would feel I had been shot through with irrelevance. Friends there would speak of these men to me all the time, as if I am a friendly aunt. I want to start again, not be an electrical rod for a previous time in my life.

The sun had mysteriously disappeared completely, and I looked out the window at the now rather grey day and at the square red-brick building across from me. There are many windows, all the same size, in this apartment building, and all of them were dark. There was not one light on. It made the building look mysterious. If I'd seen it in a photo, I might have thought I want to be sitting in an apartment looking at this building of many hidden stories.

Could I, I asked, get to the Waw from where I was sitting?

My friend was right last night. I am definitely going. I just don't know how. I am being pulled, pulled toward it, without much say in the matter. It is a hidden oasis waiting for me. But what is an oasis? A place of water where the stones have been pickaxed, rolled away. Souls have died and been riven to get to that water.

And what is water? A blessing in religious ceremonies. A cleansing agent. A refresher of soul and body. Most of us are happy in water. Children can't wait to get back in. Men do a powerful crawl when they swim in the sea, as if they are conquering. Women take baths as if being immersed in love. Many choose to die in it.

The Waw is all of that.

Chapter Nine

A Mind at Sea. My eyes fastened on that title as I looked over at my books. I knew the writer, who is now dead. A lot of dead writers around me.

I had decided to go. I couldn't help it. Last night I saw the man again, the one standing next to me looking at the small town, it wasn't him, but it was the same type. We were on a call about music, nine of us, and he separately messaged me about something I had written related to the subject. He wanted to read it or submit it to a music festival he was on the board of. After the call, I practically flew down the street to my next meeting. I was flying because I had made a new connection.

In the morning I spoke with a woman about a project that would launch me into something very different, but we held back, not knowing if we really could put ourselves out there. The night before I had spoken to a woman about another project that would also be a new journey but was so amorphous that it was almost impossible to speak about it tangibly.

Ideas, waiting to take form.

They were all paths to the sea town. None of them were full-on yet. I could say, Would they ever be? But my life, all our lives, are about making ideas tangible. I had always been up for it. I used to just find a way, heedlessly. I might have fallen over myself, but I was, unwittingly, stepping forward. Now, I was not so heedless. I cogitated, I pondered, I strategized, I weighed. This all came off as stalling. Did I need to be heedless again? It would be marvelous really to just say the hell with everything and do it.

All these projects under discussion required money, and money and I have been uneasy intimates. The buck seems to stop always there, not here. I watch money sail by me in the same way I watched an athlete's tennis balls fly by me yesterday. I should have been hitting them back, just like my arm should have been reaching toward money all these years.

I didn't bother with money when young. I just found a way to survive. This attachment to survival was all difficult and worrying and still is at times, and why was I letting it hold me back now?

I went to sleep and dreamed of Capri.

Deleuze and Guattari, the French philosophers, wrote of nomads. I glanced again at my bookcases. I saw Spinoza. Nietzsche. Miller. Markson. Belano. All the nomads of the mind. Perhaps it was why I kept them round me. They were all living, nomadically, on bookshelves. They moved away and then they moved on and then they moved here and everywhere else they wanted to be.

Chapter Ten

People bothering me, bothering me, bothering me, so I felt bad tempered and I was not used to being bad tempered. Something not right. I seemed to have exhausted everything here.

I got on a plane and left.

Chapter Eleven

The wrapping of thick silk. I stood at the arrival dock, breathing in this wide, singing salt air, which went right to my heart. I heard the seagulls cawing out estimated fishing boat arrival times. I heard a certain long silence that I had no idea I needed so much. It seemed to be rearranging my synapses to an even place.

My city apartment would just have to be silent, too. I'd go back sometime, but not till I was remade. I'd worry about the money part later, just like when I was young.

I just kept breathing. Then turned to the water, which had the sun dancing all over it, and my breath caught differently at the dazzle of it. I closed my eyes to feel even more here, and then opened them to confirm I actually was here. My phone beeped. I knocked off quick answers to a slew of Did You Get That Edit, Can You Look At This Later, and so on. I planned to keep my ship of livelihood moving, even here.

I knew I could go online to find a place to live but it didn't match the old buildings surrounding me. I wanted to novelistically walk into a shop and see an advertisement in tremulous handwriting of a place that was owned by an old person who would rent it to me, on the sea, for under value.

Still, out of habit, I pulled my phone out again from my pocket and began typing for apartments in the town.

I didn't like doing it. I felt the place should find me, not me find it. I put my phone back in my pocket.

I decided to walk around and see what street grabbed my heart. They almost all did, with their stone houses and different shapes and differently painted doors, closed tightly. Privacy is a value that I admire, and to me, privacy is now almost radical.

I turned another corner. I imagined myself finding a place that looked onto the sea, if only indirectly. A place close enough to the main street so I wouldn't feel isolated. Where I could walk to the post office, or to anything. I like to take breaks or distract myself in a coffee shop or restaurant, and I like the chance and immediate encounters when doing so. They are fodder for a spy of the heart.

I went three blocks from the main street and up a slight hill, and my eyes went to an empty dirt path that led to a house a bit back where I saw a FOR LET sign.

Not sure. But I walked up the dirt road and knocked on the door of a plain house, fairly large, and my knock was immediately responded to by a dog barking out, Who's That? I hoped his two-legged charges were home.

The door opened and it was an older woman, red hair, wearing glasses, but quite elegant, and she smiled warmly and said, in an unexpected Polish accent, "You are here for the apartment?"

"Yes, may I see it?"

She opened the door and nodded her head quickly, to come in, in that European way of "Now we do it."

"This way," she said politely and formally. I trusted her lack of seduction.

But then she turned around and walked out the very door she'd asked me to come into, instead of bringing me in, and I turned around and followed her. We went round the perimeter of the square and rather mundane house, with a few dead plants strewn about, only to surprisingly come upon a wide view of the whole harbor and the abundance of trees on the other side of it, stone houses sprinkled high up on that very hill where I had originally stood. This must be where the boats come in from the sea, I thought. I didn't care what the place she had to let looked like; I was taking it.

We walked down the hill to a little house, tiny, really, one room on top of another, what did I care. "It was a playhouse," she said. "A big one. My children liked to sleep there with their friends and have, I suppose, very interesting talks."

We entered a tall door. Inside was a desk, a chair, a ladder to a loft to sleep in, which I stepped up onto, and there lay a mattress and blankets. This little house had magnificent windows. It smelled almost new.

Looking at her, I wondered if it also was a place for her to hide if she ever had to. Maybe there was a room underneath. She was clearly a refugee.

"There is no kitchen of course, but you can use mine," she said.

"Oh, I don't cook." A comment that usually gets a questioning look, as if I am mad.

She laughed.

"No, I mean it."

"I believe you." She smiled. "Let me ask you, do you eat?"

I could feel my eyes begin to gleam. "I'll take the place."

"Don't you want to know the price?" she asked. I kept looking out the window at the water.

"Not really, but you can tell me."

The amount was equal to a dinner that I would drag myself to and maybe drink too much at because I was slightly bored at a decent restaurant in New York.

I gave her two months.

"After that?" she asked.

"We'll see," I said.

"I agree," she replied.

This was a most fortuitous landlord.

"Where are your things?" she asked.

"I left my suitcase at the landing. Is there a plug here?"

"Of course. I remember doing the same thing with a suitcase many years ago."

"What year?" I asked, knowing I shouldn't.

"What do you think?" she asked, and I nodded.

I imagined she was a child when she came. But maybe not.

"I found my second husband here. He died," she said.

"Oh, I am sorry." That "second husband" confused me timewise, but I was not here to interrogate her.

"Yes. Thank you," she said. She hesitated for a second, and then I heard, "Why, may I ask, did you come?"

"I am not sure. To begin, I do know I am looking for silence."

"Yes, America is very chaotic."

"True. But . . ." I looked out at the moving water and the colorful and sturdy harbor and pointed. "I am looking for that, and I cannot explain to you why."

I wanted to use the word infinity but that seemed a bit pretentious, even to me.

"We'll find out," I said.

"Of course," she said. "Oh, there are no keys."

"I can always put in a lock if I need to."

"Yes," she agreed. "But one doesn't need them here."

That seemed unfathomable. "I'm going down to the landing," I said.

"I'll get some sheets for you." She looked around the little house closely, as if thinking. "I'll also get you a muffin. You must be hungry after your journey."

I smiled but only to mask that I felt a bit like crying.

Chapter Twelve

I was pulling my bag along the street, I really didn't have much, I've always liked to travel light, although I had a feeling if I did need to buy something here, it would look like a throwback in time.

I also was carrying my laptop, I had brought a converter, I supposed I would have to have wireless put in, there must be someone who knew how to do that. This wasn't another planet. I found carrying my laptop always difficult, being too much of a fashionista to wear a backpack. I always thought backpacks were rude to other people. You don't know how much of their space you are taking up.

"Want me to help you?"

I turned. It was the tall man I had stood next to, when looking at this town. He had a dark pea jacket on, a knit sweater underneath. Dark eyes. A dark cap. He had gentle eyes but a strong body. He also seemed to have a sense of humor. It was interesting that it was his eyes alone that could communicate that.

"Oh, thank you," I said. "I find it hard carrying this briefcase or whatever it is. I can roll the other one easily."

He took the laptop bag and, let me say, I am always nervous when anyone touches my laptop bag. What if he runs off with it? Then I thought, Why would he? It's not like it holds the answers to world peace and eternal life.

"I just took a place up the hill," I explained.

He nodded and began walking. Once again, we were silent. I cannot tell you how pleasurable that is. I strode with a different gait since I knew where I was going but he kept up. Since he was not a talker, I took in more of my surroundings. Some of the houses were like manor houses and others were one floor but substantially wide. None overshadowed the other, which ended up creating something sort of good for the soul, with an occasional dog coming up to give or withhold approval.

We sauntered on till we came to the dirt road.

"Up here," I said. "You okay?" I asked, turning toward him. In a flash I realized my question "You okay?" was a leftover apology for asking anyone to do anything for me. Talk about betraying oneself.

He laughed. "If I can't manage this bag, I might as well give it up."

Silence can reveal a lot, I thought.

We continued up the dirt road, round the house.

He followed. Now I heard, "I didn't know Lucia has an extra place up here."

Then he saw my playhouse abode. "Good thing you're on the small side," he said.

"I guess so. I don't need more, really."

It has always been me and the laptop, I thought.

"Are there technical people," I asked, "who could put in wireless?"

"My nephew. I'll ask him. He could come round later, I would imagine."

"Great. I'll pay him."

Well, now I have everything.

He didn't come in or even come close to the door. Put the bag down outside. I liked that.

"Thanks," I said. For some reason, I did not want to know his name.

"See you." I guess it was likewise.

"Thanks again," I called out.

I opened the door. My landlady had left ivory and purple roses in a lovely grey and black vase, sheets, towels, and, to the side, a tiny microwave. I can warm up coffee. What an extraordinary woman. Intuitive and kind. I wondered if those traits go together.

I put my bags down, sat down in the one chair, looked out at the water, and thought, Now what?

Chapter Thirteen

I put the towels in the tiny bathroom. I would miss my baths, but they say showers are better for you anyway. I climbed up the ladder, carrying the sheets, to get more of a feel of the place.

She must, at eighty something, have climbed the ladder herself when she came back to drop off things for me.

She'd also left a radio. Even plugged it in. I switched it on to see what I would get. Bruckner string quartet. Delicate, interweaving, plaintive. All those different cello, viola, violin, and bass voices driving.

I lay down and listened, my eyes fastened on the sea outside.

And Bruckner took over.

Chapter Fourteen

I slept there that night, to a silence that was so deep that I thought I was out on the ocean. There was pure stillness, no fishing boats coming in, nothing. So quiet it made me wake up. The silence was that loud.

And I looked to the window and there I thought I saw a man, dark eyes, dark hair with a beard, staring in at me.

Everything in me panicked and I stayed completely still. So this is how it ends.

In the morning I told myself that it was my imagination. It was just too bizarre, and it was so Jungian. A dark man at the window. What does it mean? Is it sexual? I typed on my phone "dream a dark man at the window." It said, *If you dream this, not to fear. You have met someone who is probably pretty interesting, and you want to get to know them better.*

What a strange way for one's unconscious to communicate.

The man who carried my laptop. Obvious.

Chapter Fifteen

I went down to the dock, that one road along the water, and looked for a coffee shop. I found a ground floor place complete with a bell when you walked in and the tables were real wood with chairs that had backs that were cushioned, kind of homey, and the building had long windows over the harbor, and I sat down.

I had that excitement I get when doing something new. Something is about to happen. I looked around. It was empty, and no menus. The owner called out, "Right there, dear. Am alone here today."

"No worries."

That silence again, and I luxuriated in it. No more New York sirens, and people talking loudly to themselves on their cells as they passed you.

Then the bell rang again, and the man who'd carried my laptop walked in with a younger version of himself. He came right up to me, as if looking for me.

"I knew you'd come down here for breakfast," he said, standing over me. "That tiny place couldn't possibly have a kitchen. Anyway, this is my nephew, and he will install your wireless."

"I was just thinking about it," I said, smiling. "You two want to sit down? May I buy you a coffee? I appreciate your helping me like this."

They pulled the chairs back to sit. The owner came over. "Hi Skene. Hi Nick."

"Good morning, George," the tall man I'd met at the dock said. "This woman just moved here."

George said, "Does she have a name, or shall we make one up?"

"Make one up," I said.

George, shaggy grey hair and smiling, probably likes a few pints, said, "Well, let me see now." He stared at me. "Esmerelda."

Nick, the younger one, said, "Who's she?"

George said, "I can't remember but she has wavy hair."

Skene, the one who'd carried my laptop, said, "She was always with a clever goat, wasn't she?" He turned to me. "Did you happen to have one in your bag?"

"Where's Esmerelda from?" I asked.

"Hunchback of Notre Dame," Skene said.

George said, "That's right. Also, she's a seductive dancer."

Skene said, "Are you?"

"I don't think so."

George said, "Well, too bad about that. I'll get you two boys some coffees and scones. Do you want anything besides coffee?" he said to me.

"No thanks."

"Yanks," George said. "Coffee, coffee, coffee."

Nick said, "I thought that was South American."

George said, "Well, they at least have a medialuna with it."

Skene turned to George. "I didn't know you were versed in South American cuisine. Do you happen to have any medialunas?" he joked.

George replied, "In fact, I don't, and I'm glad to see there's a lot you don't know, Skene," and went off to get the coffees.

"What does Skene mean?" I asked him. "An unusual, lovely name."

"It's Scottish, I think for dagger, but," he added, "I doubt my parents knew that."

The sun was on the water. The coffees came pronto and the

two men relaxed a bit. Skene studied me, which made me sort of erotic to myself. God knows how I looked in reality. I hadn't thought about a mirror in that house. I'm at that age where no mirror can at times be a relief.

Nick said, "So I'll come this afternoon with a router and get you set up."

"Do I need to sign up for a service or something?"

"We'll see if you can hook on to anyone else when I get there. If not, we'll figure it out. After all, the whole world has, so we probably can."

"I agree."

"Are you on some kind of mission here? Some kind of journalist or something?" Skene asked.

"No," I said,

He didn't pursue it.

I found him a bit attractive with his dark intelligent eyes. I like tall thin men, always have. I suppose my father who was tall has something to do with it, although not thin by the time I came on the scene. I also like mystery, and men who don't talk all the time emanate that.

We finished our coffees, and all got up together. "I'm going to look around a bit," I said.

I looked to George, who waved his hand. "No charge. A welcome gift. Tomorrow I'll double your price."

"Thank you," I said.

Skene nodded, as did Nick. We all walked out together, and I went right, and they went left.

Skene was not the man at the window. He doesn't have a beard. But everything else was him in some way. Or the feeling was. Intensity. What does he do? I wondered. It's almost as if he were a mythological character, does something like take people along the river Styx.

Maybe he's a shrink.

God, I hope he's not a pastor.

He did smile at breakfast. A bit warmer than yesterday. But he seemed to be taking me in very conscientiously, which is a bit seductive. One's own power starts to fluff up out of nowhere. Is he frightened of me or attracted to me or neither?

There is a thing about being an older woman. You can't tell. You remember people attracted to you so you think they're still attracted to you when they look but, in truth, they may be thinking, Oh, what a nice woman. Must have been good-looking in her day. I wonder if she has a daughter.

In other words, you have all the same insecurities as before.

Chapter Sixteen

Skene knocked on my door two days later at about 5 pm. At least he wasn't at the window. It was a welcome intrusion because even though I was enjoying my time alone, looking out at the sea, and sort of wrestling with coming up with a film script for someone and feeling the pleasure of knowing I wouldn't have to talk about it with the producer, only send it off, I still needed a break of some sort. My back was hurting me, and I wasn't sure if it was the mattress up there or the possible idea I am self-destructive by running away like this, or, in short, I was feeling a little sorry for myself. They are right, those who say you take yourself with you.

"I hope I am not bothering you," he said, as I opened the door. He stood over me and looked sort of warm and steady, reliable. A person, I thought, not someone hiding himself. "Would you like to come out to the local here and meet some people, as well as have a drink with me?"

My answer was to turn around and look for my handbag. Then I grabbed a brown jacket I have with a tiny bit of fur on it, a gift from Kurt many years ago. Skene might mistakenly think I am rich, but who cares. I had a feeling he could give a damn one way or the other.

I climbed the ladder to turn off Mahler's Adagio in the Fifth Symphony. People think it's a love adagio, but others think it sounds like death. I'd heard it so much it was like switching off an old friend.

We walked down the hill, and it was a gentle kind of light with the sun beginning to wane, but also at the same time one could see the moon. It seemed everything was out tonight.

"Does your neck hurt you?" he asked as he trudged along.

"Yes, how did you know? I woke up with that this morning. I think it's the way I slept."

"I think it might be you hunch over a bit. With your shoulders. Try pushing them back."

I did, and it felt better.

"Are you a chiropractor?"

"No," he said. "It's just a bit obvious."

It is? I thought.

"You're right," I agreed, pushing my shoulders back. "It does alleviate some of the pain. I was hunched over my laptop yesterday for too long, I think."

"I wonder if the size of that house makes you hunch," he said.

"No, the ceiling is high," I said. "It's the damn laptop. I have never figured out the right way to sit."

He looked out over the water. "Maybe you're a bit shy."

I glanced at him, surprised. Does he mean because I sit over my laptop all the time? No, he means because I hunch, I realized, because as I was walking shoulders back now, I felt like I was a storm trooper. I realized I usually walk eyes cast down. He gave me a kind of odd smile, and then I wondered if it was maybe he who is a bit shy.

We continued on, down some streets I had never seen, more houses, to a stone building, much like the others but with an awning out front. "This place has the most ridiculous name," he said. "The Cavalier."

I didn't really care because I was busy thinking that, in some way, I felt taken care of. And I realized I had been longing for that. Perhaps it was why I left where I was in the first place.

Everyone, of course, knew everyone. It felt good being with him. He is a man, not needing expensive clothes to shout it out, not needing a Rolex, not needing an expensive haircut, a Mercedes outside. We just walked down the hill. It was so relaxing and healing. I still didn't know what he did, if anything; it would come out.

We were sitting in a quiet corner, and I was so interested in what the people were like that I just watched the laughter among men, two women speaking deeply together but also laughing, and occasionally people would come up, men and women, sort of open and friendly people, and say, "How you doing, Skene?" He'd introduce me and they'd say, "Oh you'll love it here," or something like that. Nobody said, "Watch out for him," and that was also rather pleasant. Only one person said something a bit interesting. "Have you seen his paintings?"

When that person left, I asked, "Do you paint?"

"No, no, I like paintings. I have quite a few. Some actually I inherited. My father liked them too."

"It's funny," I said. "I used to sort of be addicted to books and music, I still am, I'm sure, but paintings were like cream on a pastry. I enjoyed them when I saw them but didn't search them out. I went to the museum when someone else suggested it and I loved it, when I did, but I did not go by myself. But lately I've been finding myself more moved by paintings. The immediacy of emotion and story in a canvas, all that is said in it. I don't think I got it for a long time."

"Yes," he said. "They get to you."

"Are the paintings from around here?" I asked.

"Lots of places," he said.

I let it go.

This man might be more interesting than he lets on. Does he live alone? Nobody was saying, "Skene, how's the wife?"

He also was rather particular about the wine, when he ordered it, as if he knew about wines. I had a scotch with ginger ale. They don't put ice in it but that's all right.

I asked him what he was reading. He mentioned a writer I hadn't heard of. He said his daughter-in-law sent it to him and he ran through the book, not expecting to.

"So you have children?"

"Yes, two sons. Strangely they both work in Shanghai. I suppose after being somewhere so quiet, they decided to go somewhere the opposite."

"Interesting," I said.

How do I do this elegantly? But I didn't need to.

"My wife ran off with someone," he said. "It took me a long time to forgive myself for what I was not sure I had done. Obviously, I did something. She ended up living with a friend of mine."

"Here?"

"Not that far off. She writes me every now and then for advice."

"Sounds hard."

"It was more shocking. You don't expect that. You think you're doing the right things, taking care of the family and all, and you think you have something. I didn't know we were unhappy. As I said," and he raised his drink to his lips, "I had to really look into myself to figure it out. Took me a long time."

"Don't tell me you really did figure it out? Seems like it would be unfigurable."

"Well, there's that. You're right. But what I saw surprised me. After it happened, it's been a while, you know, I have stayed alone. Of course, the town and every town about here wants to introduce me to someone and people introduce themselves to me since it is natural to couple, I suppose, but what I find interesting is I had no desire for it. Perhaps whatever that is inside me is what she ran away from. Now I think it was."

I found myself in the odd position of identifying with both him and his estranged wife. Like him, I was surprised to find out I have a bent toward the solitary, but conversely, like his wife, I had run to find something new.

"Maybe we're all running to and away," I said.

"Maybe. But she ran to the 'away' part. I found I wasn't that interested in running 'to' so quickly. Plenty of men told me I should be."

"Because they'd like to if they were in that situation," I said. "Or they think they would."

"Of course."

Fact was he was a little twisted up inside, awkward, but also he wanted to connect in some way, he just didn't know what the hell he was doing. I sipped my drink, telling myself once again it wasn't that bad without ice.

"Of course," he said, "there is the interesting question of why you are here."

"Yes, my new landlord asked the same thing."

"Lucia? She's lovely."

"I agree."

"What did you tell her?"

"Same as your answer about your wife. It's going to take me a while to figure it out."

He nodded.

"What do you think it is?" I asked, joking. "You're good on anatomy. Maybe you're good on this stuff too."

He laughed.

"I don't know much at all. It's a funny, if beautiful, place you've chosen to come to. I wonder if you'll miss the city."

"I don't know. All I know is I had to get away."

"Might be a thing with women, this running away business," he said.

Chapter Seventeen

Nick had connected me to wireless. It turned out Lucia had it in her house, and surprisingly when we went up there to get some information, she mentioned that she was on YouTube, which I looked up when I finally got online and there were quite a few videos of her speaking about a book she'd written about her life during and post-Holocaust. Apparently, she has prophetic dreams. I couldn't understand what she was saying about them; they were full of biblical symbols and interpretations that were very detailed and relied on knowledge of Hebrew and ancient cryptologies, but even not understanding them, I fully believed whatever message she was getting in these dreams were authentic, and that she might really have a direct communication with the spirit, whatever that was.

It didn't seem like someone like her would be a trickster. Maybe she is a prophet. It was unlike me to think something like that, I am a skeptic foremost, but here, I just thought, I happen to have encountered a biblical prophet, as if I had just met a mailman.

The town may have seemed like an anachronism, but it appeared, so far, that all the dramas of life were fully going on here, as elsewhere. In some ways that disappointed me, I had been looking for what I had never known, but at the same time, it felt reassuring that I had remained connected to the planet.

Skene's paintings. Should I put them into the film I am writing?

No. Keep this life out of your writing, I told myself. Stay separate.

But isn't that what you are running from? I asked myself. The way you stay separate. Skene had held my elbow as he walked me home last night and I found it profoundly confusing. There was something lovely about being held, so to speak, about someone touching me, something soothing and safe about it, but also something terrifying. Perhaps that is why I am here, I began to think. To confront how I stay away, although here I was, having gone away to focus on staying away.

I climbed up the ladder and began a book by a woman who mentioned a blind spot. As she defined it, it is where you do yourself in, but are not aware of it. She apparently can regress people to where they see how their blind spot originated. The writer claims you make some agreement with yourself as a child and never get over it. Mine was at age three or four. My mother pushed me away and I said to myself, in child language, "If you want to survive this, don't attach or expect anything." Oddly or predictably, I proceeded to approach all my relationships for the rest of my life using that philosophy, in work and love. Don't expect anything, and don't attach. It inhibited my career because I could never ask for anything and it hindered my love life for, as soon as I got involved, I was thinking how to get uninvolved.

This trait has landed me here, I now realized, although, as I thought that, I wasn't exactly clear on why I thought that.

I was no better than Skene's wife, I knew that much. I was good at going, so I should be careful with his heart. Never mind mine.

Then I heard a knock downstairs. I must say, I preferred it to a phone.

I climbed down the ladder.

There I saw Skene through the window. In a way that made me feel less lonely here. He didn't seem needy since there was no preening, but it showed he does want contact. And that thought had me once again frightened.

"Hope I am not bothering you," he said.

"Not at all."

"I thought you might want to come over and see the paintings. At your convenience, of course."

"Sure." I went to my phone to look at the time. 2:30. "How about around 6 pm?" I asked.

"Fine. I'll pick you up."

"Great."

Then he turned around and left.

I did put on a nicer blouse, a polka-dot one I kind of liked, black and white with a ruffle and long sleeves, a bit sheer but not enticing, and I wondered if I should invite him in for a drink but that seemed a bit odd. If we sat down, we'd be practically on top of each other, so, when he arrived, I just closed the door and stepped out.

We began walking down the hill and said nothing to each other, as usual, which I still found to be a kind of elixir. I was taking in the view, of course, of the grey water and intermittent trees next to it and the bridge running across the harbor, all of it lovely, and there was no way really to respond to that, except to take it in. We did not walk to the main street but stayed high up on the hill and continued along the road for about ten minutes till we came to a tall stone house.

"Used to be a priory," he said to the sound of a dog barking inside. "Oh, that's George. He thinks he's a lapdog but he's enormous. A lab. Friendly though, so don't be frightened. Maybe not that intelligent."

The door opened and George came wagging his tail out to see who Skene was with. He was pleased, I surmised, that at least I'd brought his master home, so, even though he was far from a collie, he began herding us inside.

The house was furnished very pleasantly and sparsely, a fireplace in the living room, a dining room, a big kitchen, and then an upstairs and downstairs that I didn't see.

"I'll get you a scotch," he said.

I followed him into the kitchen, which was neat and tidy, and he said, "Ice? You're American," and I nodded.

Then he poured himself the same thing.

He said, "Ready?" handing me my drink.

And he led the way.

First, I saw a de Chirico. Dark with greens. I said nothing. I remember once visiting a doctor and he had paintings of so many great artists, his collection would have to have been worth millions and millions, and I decided that the doctor's paintings were copies. Nobody had that many paintings. He even had an alleged El Greco and I thought, How can he even have the right lighting to protect it?

I didn't feel these here were fakes, and there weren't as many. Some seascapes, portraits, one by Dali of a businessman, was it tongue in cheek, I wondered. I tended to like the seascapes, many by people I did not know, and there were many interesting paintings—in the living room, and across from the dining room.

I wanted to ask, "How do you come to have these?" but then I didn't want to. He wasn't saying how. He didn't seem like an art thief, but then a good thief wouldn't.

He looked like a sea captain.

I sat down after and said nothing except, "Exquisite. Truly exquisite."

I looked around. Books. Mostly British history.

I didn't feel a woman's presence, although it wasn't a messy place. But that could be a cleaning lady or himself.

He kept studying me as I was looking around. Did he think I was a painting?

"What are you looking at?" I asked.

"You."

"Why?"

"It's so pleasant to see someone in this town who looks so out of place."

I decided that was kind of a compliment. He too must long for something different.

"We all know each other, for years," he said. "Families. All of it. It's comforting in a way, and we can rally together when needed, but also it can be a bit . . . the same."

"Yes," I said, "I would imagine."

Something made me sad at that moment. Perhaps the loneliness there with the paintings.

A man alone with his paintings.

Maybe he could not break through his aloneness, like I couldn't.

Was my loneliness as hard to witness as it was to witness his? I think I was more defended, going about here, there, and everywhere. But I remembered how I used to pity people who were alone, pitied them while knowing deep down I was going to be one of them.

I turned to him and smiled.

"That's better," he said.

Chapter Eighteen

Lucia never knocked on my door. This was profoundly interesting. Aren't elderly widows always looking for company? Not her. She was never about.

Her life must be full, in her mind, I got the feeling.

Maybe everybody's here was.

Kurt used to always say to me when I would see some small town, or sweet neighborhood that looked intriguing, he'd pipe up, "But what would one do here?"

I didn't understand it. What does one do anywhere? One works, reads, loves, has dinner, watches movies, socializes, plays sports. One does those everywhere.

If we were discussing a holiday, he would say, "But what will we do there?"

Yet when we had gone on holiday, he only wanted to play sports, read, have dinner.

I too had always been the busy type, going to this and that, and then it became almost exhausting and I saw that people not doing that had just as full lives. I exclude live music from this because there should always be live music. And theater, now that I think about it. And film, of course.

But there is just as vivid a life without it. The mind invents.

Lucia, it seemed, just needed her own mind, and judging from her YouTube videos, she spends her time conversing with God.

Some people, of course, are put in loony bins for that. Looking off at her shuttered house that she mysteriously emerges now and then from to leave me chocolates or fig bars, her intimacy with God seemed perfectly right, thriving and important.

I was working happily by myself, my mind not with God but with ideas and words, which is my kind of happiness, more so than any other, even love, and I needed to get up and walk. My body pays for it when I don't.

I went down the hill and was facing a house on another cove with a beautiful balcony over it and people were going in and out. I didn't skulk alongside them, but I did sort of, and wanted to see what they were like. Suddenly Skene said, "Do you want to go in there?"

"What's going on?" I asked, as if it were normal for him to turn up unexpectedly. It had indeed become a bit normal at this point.

"It's a condolence party. This woman's husband died."

"Oh. Well, I don't know them, it would be a bit strange if I go in."

"They're as interested in you as you are in them," he said.

I looked at him, his deep dark eyes, and found myself temporarily immobilized. Then, as always, I decided to move forward.

There was a huge assortment of freshly made food on a table and the new widow was a round, quick-moving, smiling woman in her eighties, I guessed. She had large intense, intelligent brown eyes and a beautiful smile. I said, "I am so sorry even though I never met your husband. I was just walking by."

She said, "Yes, I've been wondering about you. I hope you are comfortable here."

"Oh yes, very. Thank you."

A Filipino nurse came up to me, dressed in red slacks and a black sweater and a very expensive Hermès belt, which I only recognized because Kurt had once tried to get me interested in such, and she apparently was taking care of the new widow. She was a kind of daughter-in-law, I eventually figured out. Suddenly we were all sitting around, Skene had disappeared once he saw I was comfortable. Was he outside? Gone? The older woman was full of humor and pragmatic, missed having a husband, she'd always had one, she said. She is not independent, she told everyone who told her how independent she is. "I just look that way. I'm not at all. I don't know how to put gas in a car. I didn't pay the bills. I don't know how to put the heat on."

"People can do that for you," her brother said, an older man who seemed to command everyone's respect. Avuncular and witty.

Then the conversation went to friends of hers who had met men at her age and either married them or were together living separately.

"Like me," the brother said. "Penelope and I don't live together."

Penelope, sitting on the other side of the room, shot him a look of bemusement. Obviously, the brother said that to needle her.

"Yes," the widow said, "I don't want to marry again. I've buried two husbands. It's difficult as they age, and things happen. But one does want to have someone to talk to, do things with."

Then she turned to me, "You're here alone."

"Yes," I said.

A silence, as if I was to explain it.

In answer: "I had someone where I came from, but he said he wasn't in love with me and I don't know, for some reason that made me run away, I guess."

And the way they all nodded their heads, I began to think, Maybe that is the reason I left. But I didn't really think it was.

Till Skene piped up—What is he? An apparition? "Maybe he is in love with you and doesn't know it," he said.

The widow said, "Skene, it is something one knows about oneself."

"Not everyone," he said. "What do you think?" He addressed me.

"I think you do know. You think you can't live without this person. You may regret thinking that a bit later when you know them better and think you probably can live very well without them but then you realize, in reality, you can't live without them."

"You may have to," the widow said.

"Yes. And even if he doesn't know, but is in love with me, he is still acting like he isn't. You want someone to act like he is. So that is what I mean, I think."

"What is acting like one is in love like?" Skene asked.

Nobody said anything to that.

The widow said, "Skene, why are you so interested in this?"

I answered him anyway. "Being in love creates a moving forward," I said. "You want to invent and build something with the person. It's creative and you do something new."

My mind flashed to the nomads in the desert. They move within the desert. They know how to sustain themselves. They know where their sources are. Where they can find an oasis, not a mirage.

The widow poured me a weak Bloody Mary and I was glad it was weak.

"Well, I'm happy I got to know you," the widow said.

"And I, you."

"You can stop in if you are lonely. I probably will be."

I looked around at her attentive family and thought, I don't think that's going to be as true she thinks. In my case, an open issue.

"You're in Lucia's tiny house, right?" someone said.

I nodded.

"Lucia hardly ever comes out. Charming woman when she does, but she is not very social."

I thought that might be the best way to live in a place like this. "She wrote a book, you know," another person said, "*The Rose Temple.*"

"I couldn't understand a lot of it," someone else said.

"That could be said of Shakespeare," a fourth said.

Skene smiled at that, and I looked over at him and smiled too. There was something lively about all this. And something comforting about how he had managed, in some way, to align him and me together.

Chapter Nineteen

I was listening to and staring out at the sea from my little house and, things being what they are, my mind went to sex. I had noticed in the last year I had begun to recoil when being touched. It was confusing to me. As if I did not want any expectations at all put on me and yet being touched is supposed to be about pleasure. But I didn't feel that. I felt invaded.

For many years Kurt would not touch me, and I fretted about it. Am I too old to be touched? Is he longing for someone else? And, like a tree slowly being cut down, I quelled my desire, my sap. I shut myself down to a stump.

Then, all of a sudden, after years of me not expecting it, of learning to live without it, he began to want to touch me, and I didn't know what to do.

I remembered a lover saying to me once on a public beach, albeit an enclave, "Do me." I was shocked and thought, Do what? Although I knew what he wanted, but when someone tells me to do something, my mind goes blank.

Then I thought about Kurt in the past few months. He would wake me and pull hard at my arm and hand to rub him, and I resented being woken that way. Why not caress me so I wanted, of my own volition, to rub his penis? It all sort of made me contrary, which I am, anyway.

If you tell me to pull up the brim of my hat, I might be inclined to pull it down. That was the thing I admired about the sub-Saharan nomads. They would not be colonized. When they were forced to be, it was a time of longing and sadness.

Kurt would leave me articles that said that giving a woman oral sex gives men cancer. While he was leaving these articles for me by the bedside, I deduced his current warming up to me as "cosmetic." While he was staying away from my nether parts, I spent time reading novels written by men who spent long passages on love scenes pleasing a woman. They considered it part of the act. I read of no deaths through this form of being loving.

I swung my legs over the ladder to come down. Yes, this place is a bit small once you live in it and it did have the effect of making one feral. I needed to go outside to feel any sense of space.

I suppose it was, in that sense, the perfect place for someone to be in transit all the time.

But my tiny window upstairs almost created a picture frame for the water and the buildings, a painting, and I paid homage to it every time I looked outside.

I had told Skene I like to play tennis and he told me of a place apparently about six roads away. Today I decided to walk over. He'd said someone would give me a racquet when I got there.

It was a bit cool, and the walk was beautiful with the trees, houses, gardens next to the water held in the light, but I did not see anyone as I walked. Not even a car. It was like Brigadoon when everyone slept for a hundred years.

Palace of Books Tennis and Racquet Club. I reread it about four times. Someone must have a sense of humor.

I went in and could hear the metronome of balls hit back and forth in indoor courts adjacent to the waiting room. An Asian woman smiled.

I said, "I've just moved here and I don't know if it's possible but I would like to play with someone at some time. I am not that good but passable."

"Oh," she said, "we are just having a clinic now. You could go in and find someone."

"Great," I said. "I don't have a racquet."

She produced one.

She walked me to a court where there were three young female players, and a very old man who, surprisingly, was somewhat august and in good shape who stood tall and straight like a Roman senator. He nodded hello and it seemed I was to play with him.

He volleyed well and was pleasant to hit with. I would apologize when the ball went off, for instance, into the next court but he would just say, "Oh don't worry about that. Come on then."

Then it seemed the clinic was over. It was not that the Roman senator and I had spoken much but I liked his directness on the court. We just played.

As we came off the court, he asked me my name and said he had heard I had moved into Lucia's little house, which he hoped was not a hotbox. "No, it isn't," I said.

"Are you happy here?" he asked.

"Yes," especially so talking to him, I thought. It is good to talk to someone you have decided you respect. It raises the level.

It turned out he was a scholar of sort, not surprising, and had written quite a bit, but the thing is, he said, "I am trying to put my papers together. I have to hire someone."

My natural inclination is, as we know, to jump into everything, but sorting someone's papers is my idea of hell, even though I found him interesting, so I uncharacteristically did not offer. However, I was curious.

"Yes, well, it's not a lot. Just sort of putting some order into them."

"I would offer," I said, "but I am not orderly. There are people really gifted at that and I am not one of them."

He smiled at me, with his strong patrician face. "Yes, it is a bit of a bore, isn't it, which is why I haven't done it properly myself." He was regal in some way. His mind. But I also thought he probably was very historical and exact and, if I really knew him, I might find him a bit confining mentally. Similar to a tennis ball, my mind likes to bounce about.

"You were very nice to play tennis with," I said. "The ball always returns in a very peaceable way."

He laughed.

"Well," he said, when we got to the front, and he put out his hand to shake mine, "very enjoyable to meet you. I am sure I will either run into you or we could play again here."

I was a bit disappointed he didn't set up a game but maybe that was my city ways, "Seize it, let's jump on it." He did not go into any changing room but walked up to a hook in the waiting area and pulled off a navy jacket and simply put it on over his grey jersey and left the place.

I turned to the Asian woman.

"You'll never guess," she said.

I thought she was going to tell me he was living with Melania Trump or something, but she said, "He is amazing, isn't he?"

"Yes," I said. Something was strong and clear in him, and because of that I liked playing with him, for that alone. It wasn't the tennis balls, and then I heard her say, "He's a hundred, you know."

A hundred what? A hundred-aire?

Apparently, she could read my befuddlement. "A hundred years old," she said.

I was so shocked that I said, "Oh. And he plays tennis."

It was as if she'd said he's a woman. The way the earth shifts a bit when what you think is, isn't at all.

"Well, I hope to see him again," I said, leaving, "as well as you."

"Just pop in when you want to play. There's always someone here to play with."

"Will do. Thanks."

As I walked back, I felt that post-exhilaration of running for and hitting balls, and I also kept thinking, "A hundred."

And how the fullness in himself and the dignity made things seem whole.

How had he not weakened?

It was almost unreal.

Chapter Twenty

No matter where you go, a swath of bills always manages to find you. I was, as always, working all the time to keep the wolf, now two of them, one in the city and one here, at bay. My work is other people's stories. It exhausts me because most of them are about conflicts, as they should be. Just some people want to write but don't want to say what the conflicts are. Don't want to go there. I can't blame them. Some people try to be funny (and usually aren't since they use the same cultural tropes everyone else does), or others minutely reveal every detail, from what they swept up off the floor to each person they've had sex with, and while some stories are more interesting than others, it all feels like one primal scream of hundreds of voices following me about.

Music is my antidote. It both soothes me and keeps me present and hence stops me from slipping irrevocably into madness.

Most of these people I read will never be writers, they just want whatever happened in their lives to be heard and understood. This also is natural and actually healthy. Real writers want the same, but they are also interested in craft, language, metaphor. They actually consider the responsibility to the reader, but the talkers talkers talkers, just the sadness of their necessity to be heard, has me at times lying back in defeat on my upstairs mattress.

Did I think I was running from them? I probably thought I would elevate myself into some new way of thinking where I couldn't do it anymore and something else would come along. Like working part time at that tennis club? Which would not afford two wolves at the door.

I never had trouble understanding how people married for money. I just had trouble understanding how they could bear it for more than two days if it was only for money. Hard enough bearing someone you are in love with.

I was a bit tired since Skene yesterday had popped over and suggested I might want an evening where I could actually have room to stretch my legs out in front of me, and he was going to watch Hitchcock's *Stranger on a Train*. I had never seen it and he was right, I was a bit in need of more cubic feet.

We sat in his living room, and I admired that his walls were a certain elegant grey with white trim. There was something intelligent about that. Maybe a homage to the view. We drank some white wine, ate nuts, and watched the film. I was amazed at the artistry of it and the talent of the writers and the actors. Because it is a thriller, it was hard to know if it is great art, but it certainly was made with almost perfect direction.

Raymond Chandler had been one of the scriptwriters. La Jolla had been his Waw. He had a house overlooking the sea and one journalist came over and looked out his window at the Pacific in the setting red sun and burst into tears. That journalist might have been seeing his own Waw.

Skene and I sat appropriately separate for two people of our age and ambivalence about a relationship.

Once the film was finished, and we marveled about it, and I looked up on my phone if it had won any awards, I got ready to go. I knew I had work waiting at home, but I would have jumped up in any case.

"I can walk you," he said.

"I know the way now."

"Don't be ridiculous."

And, as he stood up, and was letting me leave without any fuss, I felt warmly toward him. His masculinity was a bit entrancing, but I did not want to touch him. It was so long since I had wanted to touch someone in that way where your hands don't even ask you. I had liked to touch Kurt. But it had been so long since it had been a matter of survival to touch someone. Actually, when I had touched Kurt, it felt good but somehow it felt like I couldn't break through, I couldn' t rest in that touch. He would move away or make funny sounds to distract himself from the possibility of intimacy.

Skene put his coat on.

We walked to my place in the dark, a slightly clouded moon on the water.

"Today I played tennis," I said, "and I met a man who apparently is a hundred years old but there he was playing tennis. He was my partner. I am still in shock."

"Oh, yes, that's Sir Leo."

"How is it he is a hundred and . . . like he is."

"Power of the mind, I suppose. And good genes or good fortune. Maybe happiness. I don't know. He's a very nice man. Keeps to himself, writes books on music. I can't read them, you have to be a scholar to understand them, but he's engaging when you socialize with him."

"Is he married?"

"No. Maybe he was. I don't know. He's been alone since I've known him. Perhaps that's the secret of his longevity." He gave me a sidelong glance.

"In the States, they say the opposite. Married people live longer."

"They say a lot of things in the States," he said.

I chuckled. "They do." We passed a house where I noticed four sheep watching us in the garden. I was so thrilled that I dropped my purse, but Skene kept walking, so I picked it up and caught up with him. Then I said, out of the blue, the sheep perhaps inspiring me, although they were a lot sweeter than what I was about to go on about, "One of the things that has shocked me lately and may be a reason I am here is I discovered there are so many sheep in the States. They have a congress member who suggested a ministry of truth. I thought the States was the beacon for freedom. I doubt that person's read Orwell. Maybe it's why I left. The government is starting to want to silence certain people, who say what they don't like to hear. It's not like they never had idiots before but now there is a right and wrong speech as deemed by each party. Then the news only reports what they think their party wants, not the actual news. It's like *Pravda*."

"What's that got to do with Sir Leo?"

"Nothing," I said. "You're right." We'd reached my place by now. "Thank you for a lovely time," and I kissed him on the cheek and then ran into my place, as if I was about to cry or, rather, because I was going to cry.

I felt heartbroken. Was it about the moon on the water? The poignancy and possibility of a person being a hundred and vital? Was it about the potential loss of what the States had always been a beacon for? The image of integrous freedom, a freedom you could trust. The loss of that in everyone's unconscious? Was it about being walked home in the quiet?

Or was it just much simpler, about a man being kind and gentle and patient with me?

Chapter Twenty-One

Kurt sent me emails every now and then. About his grandson. How he was "having a ball," whatever that meant. He asked me if I was finding what I was looking for.

What do you think I am looking for? I wrote.

No idea. Don't you know?

At that, I got up and switched on the radio. Mahler's first movement of the Ninth. The section that sounds like a boat rowing languidly, the oars moving repetitively, sonorously, then the discordance of rocks and danger and people's souls arguing, but then back to the lilting, the lilting, lilting, of the rowing and the water and the movement.

Not sure, I wrote. The violins were now soaring at the rowing, the continuation of it.

Well, I hope you find it.

I wanted to write him that I wouldn't. Didn't he know that? I had just come here so I could hear the sound of the rowing.

Chapter Twenty-Two

Woke up, put on the radio as I always do, Vivaldi's Sacred Music. I never really liked it that much but I once had a lover, perhaps the most tortured of my lovers, who managed to reach the most tortured parts of myself which was perhaps the reason I got involved with him in the first place, these tortured parts returning us to those places that are burning and most alive that then become compulsive and, sadly, a bit addictive, but it can be a path to knowing what really hurt us in our lives. Anyway, he gave me a CD of Vivaldi's Sacred Music because he loved it so. He would give me a picture book of Venice since it was his favorite city, novels he loved like *The Last of the Just*, because they meant so much to him—these gifts, to him, were him giving himself to me. And they probably were. I would be frightened of the intensity.

Time proved out I was to be right when I found him waiting for me on my apartment steps at any hour of the night, when he slashed a painting I had from another man, when he pulled my hair on the street, when he showed up at strange places and when he called me terrible names and would slap me. Not hurtfully but to scare me.

But what frightened me even more was that there I would be the next day, knocking on his door to see what would happen next. I so much wanted the tender, crying out places in me to come alive, have their voice. Somehow, he had brought them out of hiding.

I looked out the window. The mist had covered everything.

That man was broken and so was I, at the time. Yet, in all that pain we were calling up in ourselves, I knew we were healing each other, going, as we did, right to early wounds. Finally, we could not stand it anymore and both of us went off to live fairly sane lives, if you could call doing this sane.

I climbed down the ladder.

I did not turn off the radio, it was as if I wanted to come to peaceable terms with this music, which has the usual bowing and curtsying of Vivaldi.

In the night, I had dreamed of sections of books I was writing only to wake up and find I wasn't writing these books at all.

Lucia and I had never even discussed heat, it escaped both our minds. Today I was missing it, wearing a sweater as I worked.

What I am trying to say is that I was left alone in a bit of a drafty edifice with just me and music right now. No projects to warm me up.

And I didn't care, for some reason.

The weather today was too inclement to go outside. There were no messages on my phone. The Sacred Music still playing. The silence around it so deep I could almost touch it. I had tried to read in the night the sort of philosophical-psychoanalytical French writer, Guattari; he was writing about desire. He promoted David Cooper's aegis of making love everywhere as opposed to getting involved in discourse. Then Guattari went on to propose that "perhaps is it necessary to clarify that 'making love' is not restricted to interpersonal relations. There are all kinds of ways to make love: one can make it with flowers, with science, with art, with machines, with social groups . . . Once the personological framework of Oedipal sexuality is shattered, a nonhuman transsexuality is established in the social realm, that is to say, through a multiplicity of material and semiotic fluxes."

Yes, we know this is so French, the intellectualism that can at times be impenetrable, but I was intrigued because years ago I had gone to a dinner party in a most beautiful house on a cliff by the sea in South America, and a night or so later, I dreamed that I returned there in a pitch-black night, could see nothing, not even the sea, and did not go into the house but made love with a plant.

I worried about myself once I had this dream.

But reading Guattari, I wondered if, late in life, I'd broken the framework, as he calls it, of Oedipal sexuality—I no longer had to be with the father and instead had gone on to "a multiplicity of material."

I had adored my father, and he gave me the gift of his being such a proponent of freedom that he did not try to control my life in any way. He was too busy dealing with his own out-of-control life. But my father was handsome, debonair, kind, and riddled with inexplicable demons that made him unrelatable and unreliable to women and real life, and maybe, I just realized as I thought about this, the being out in the black night might have been being with him anyway.

He had been in continual flux.

What was for me to trust, then, but a plant?

These Frenchmen believed that the Oedipus theory of sexuality is passé. That now we deal with the machine of media, product influences, in other words, the capitalist machine, that our material is much more than Mommy and Daddy.

It's probably why I find myself in a drafty house far away from everything, away, I suspect now, from influences of any sort. So far away from everything so I can find and make love with my own machine, as Deleuze and Guattari call it, of my material, as it drives and thrashes on.

Chapter Twenty-Three

Yesterday I walked by the town and the sea and its beauty was almost heartbreaking, the light and the small houses, and the hill and green and different colors, but, internally, I felt as if I was on a fast train going by it, taking me away from where I was longing for. I couldn't seem to stop it.

I turned around and went to the tennis club.

"Is Sir Leo about?"

"No," she said, "he is not here."

"Can you tell him that I would like to invite him for a—"

He walked in. "Oh," I said.

"Do you want to play tennis?" he asked.

I was not in tennis clothes. "No, I came here to leave you a message."

He smiled. "What is the message, dear?"

"I am not making a pass at you or anything—"

"I wouldn't think so, at my age."

"But I was wondering if we could meet for a drink and talk sometime."

He hesitated. I saw he is a man who protects himself from wasting his time.

"We can," he said, slowly. "But it might be better if you came round to my place. I don't like to go out at night."

"All right, thanks."

"Are you going to help me with my papers?" he asked.

"Probably not, but I'll help you find someone. See you then."

It did kind of disturb me that he, like all men, wanted me to provide some service.

I stomped home and knocked on Lucia's door. I had not seen her, not even her muffins. No answer.

As I walked down the hill to my tiny house, I thought maybe she refuses to be at everyone's beck and call.

What would it be like not to be at everyone's beck and call?

We're taught to be there for each other. Establish trust. Kindness. Generosity. Give. It all sounds wonderful, but what if it takes away your lifeblood? I suppose balance is the thing. That's what they all say, but balance doesn't take into context the flow of life. Sometimes life calls for more of you than usual. You tell yourself this giving away of yourself is a learning experience, and it is, I suppose.

I think I am just mad at aging. Time shortening.

At the end of the race, Diogenes said, you break into a burst of speed.

Maybe that was what I wanted to speak to Sir Leo about but not with words.

Chapter Twenty-Four

Friday rolled around and I found out from George's coffee shop where Sir Leo's place was.

"Going up there, then?" George asked.

"Yes."

"He keeps to himself, mostly."

"Yes."

"Well, you seem that type, too."

"Yes." I hesitated a bit, then said, "Did you always live here?"

"No," he said, "I come from Torquay. But my wife, she lived here. I met her at a dance and, being English, immediately insulted her as a way of saying I liked her, and one thing led to the other and I have never insulted her since, or rather, got away with insulting her. She wanted to stay this close to her family, and I thought, why not? So, I moved here as a lad. I had a job up the ironworks for a while, and then I opened this."

"Well, you seem well suited to this. Our gain."

"Mine too," he said.

On my way out of High Street, I bought a mirror so I could arrange myself for tonight.

As I prepared, I could see the sadness in my eyes. I seemed harsher than I remembered. Is this about getting older, I asked myself again. Am I angry about that? Are we all angry about that?

At 5:30, I walked along the shore, and it was a beautiful night. The red sun was starting to come down and it was lighting everything and the quiet had its own music and I started to feel better. I had called this meeting with Sir Leo, and I could not remember why I had done it. Well, I will just tell the truth. Everyone always enjoys that, except, perhaps, the person doing it.

It was a longer walk than I expected and as I walked farther and farther—he must walk this to and from the tennis court, I realized, not exactly popping round the corner—the cog lifted a bit. My hair flapped around me, and I started to feel young. I started to feel excited. Not so much about Sir Leo but because I was feeling the freedom of being out and about. I began to hope I wasn't even close to his home. The area got prettier the more I walked, hilly, and there were many ponds along the way, and integrated love affairs of white and black ducks, and gardens everywhere, with a special wildness that only comes from close tending, and space, there was space everywhere, and I became positively gay.

I should rent around here, I thought. Maybe it's living in a box that is doing me in.

Sir Leo's large estate was traditionally English, a beautiful manor house, with red brick as opposed to the grey brick everywhere else in town. Tall aristocratic cypresses, like him, as I walked toward the house, and the closer I got, I saw long windows like doors on the house.

Am I the man with the beard looking in?

He must have seen me walking since he opened the door as soon as I got to the end of the drive.

"Come in. Tell me your name again."

"Mira."

"You know mine, right."

"Yes, the tennis woman told me."

"Come sit in the drawing room." It made me think how my brother and I had visited Ben Johnson's house and I learned that the drawing room came from the expression "the withdrawing room." I would say to Kurt, "Come bring your coffee into the withdrawing room."

"What would you like to drink?" he asked.

"A vodka with tonic. Thank you."

He had the bottles, in glass crystal decanters with silver name tags on them, on a silver tray near the seating area. There were large paintings, and what surprised me was that they were abstract and strong. One was dark with white and grey and some orange as the front story. It was, as they say, explosive, and I stared at it and he said, "The Ambiguities."

I stood as he made each of us the same drink. I studied him, in his black trousers, blue shirt, all men wear blue shirts to look younger and they do seem to work for some reason. His hair was a bit sparse, but his eyes were a fierce dark. I looked around more, at the velvet couches, the Persian rugs, a woman getting out of a bath in one picture, and lamps about that had slender and graceful bases. Then I saw a tall Oriental vase with a tennis racquet sticking out of it, as if it were a large flower. Amused, I turned to him.

"So, what made you come to our little hamlet?" he asked.

"I keep thinking about that myself. At first, I thought it was 'silence' or the sea I was looking for, but now I think I wanted to get away from the culture I was living in."

"What do you mean?" he asked.

"The headlines that sound like gladiator rallies, the business of celebrity, I wanted to clear my mind. Other times I think I came because I am trying to figure out what love is, and other times I think I might be having a breakdown."

"Or a breakthrough," he said.

"That would be nice," I said.

"Well, it probably is what is going on. To what we don't know."

"No."

I wasn't sure what to say next. "Did you find someone to help you with your papers?"

"No, but maybe I don't want anyone. Obviously, I could advertise, and I can't be bothered with the interviews. I must be ambivalent about putting them in order."

"It's hard to have someone go through your things."

"Especially when you're alive," he said.

I smiled. "Well, thank God you happen to be. It would be quite a boring cocktail hour without you."

"'Happen to be' might be the operative words."

"Actually," I said, "you might be the only hundred-year-old in the world who plays tennis."

"We'll never know . . . maybe there is a Himalayan playing at a hundred and ten."

I thought, This is really pleasant, sitting in this large drawing room. I could feel myself relaxing. He got up and left the room for some reason, and I was struck that there was no creakiness, no bending as he moved, and then he returned with some shrimp in a large dark green bowl with ice.

"That's so kind of you," I said.

"My pleasure." He smiled. Was he flirting? "So, what did you want to discuss with me?" he asked, smiling. "I hope it's good."

He also had a deep voice for an old man.

"To be honest, I don't remember. I've been thinking so many things being in my own company all the time that I get on internal rants and whatever it was that made me search for you has passed. Forgive me."

"Not at all. I'm very glad you're here. It's unusual having this polite storm of a woman showing up out of nowhere."

It was strange to hear myself so described but perhaps not inaccurate.

"Do you live alone here?" I asked.

"Yes, except for people coming in and out to help me with this and that about the house."

"Were you married?"

Then I suddenly thought he might be gay, and here I was asking him a ridiculous question.

"Yes, of course I was. She died when I was ninety. A lad."

"Oh, I am so sorry."

"Then I bought this place and moved here because I too wanted to be in this hamlet, once I saw it, and I didn't want to be where we had been."

"You mean you left your friends and family?"

"Didn't you?" he asked.

"Yes, but . . ."

"It doesn't matter how old you are. Maybe I wanted to do one more unusual thing before I . . . do the most usual thing."

"Has coming here lived up to your hopes?" I asked.

"I don't know. I think so."

That was an English answer. A New York one would be a complaint.

Then I said, "Did you ever see dead fishermen in the harbor?"

"No. Why? Have you? Are you with the police or something?"

"No, not at all. But I had a very strong vision of it when looking at the water."

"Odd."

"I think it was just a symbol in my mind for death."

"Your imagination, you mean?"

"Yes."

He looked at me and I assumed at this point he was wondering if I was mad.

"I don't think I'm mad," I said to his unspoken thoughts, "perhaps just too . . ."

"If it is imaginative you are about to say," he interrupted, "that is a wonderful thing, my dear. You should be grateful. Much good has come into the world through imagination."

I wasn't quite sure what he was saying but it was a sweet compliment, whatever it meant.

"Well," he said, "shall we have dinner?"

"Oh, I wasn't expecting that," I said.

"Doesn't matter. I've had it all set up. The cook is here. Come along to the dining room."

Off we went to a blue dining area, everything beautifully set, and gorgeous wine glasses with a white wine chilling, and I sat down next to him, and an older woman came out with a leek soup.

"Very healthy," he said.

"Good, too," I added, after he'd poured the wine and we began.

"What do you do," he asked me, "for work?"

"I write books and things."

"Are they any good?"

"I don't know. They're a little avant garde."

"Not a huge surprise."

"I don't think you'd like them. I'm frightened to reread them myself."

"Understood."

Really? I thought.

"And now what?"

I hadn't had this fluid a conversation in years. He had to be a nomad himself.

"I don't know," I replied. "What do you suggest I write next?" I asked as a joke.

"Have another glass of wine," he replied.

That was a good answer. In truth, I hate when people tell me what I should write except for the fact you learn a little about the people giving advice.

Kurt's last suggestion was that a writer's boyfriend writes a best seller and she has to deal with it. Quite telling.

I looked across at Sir Leo. Imagine picking up at his age. Going through a new door. The creativity and risk of it.

"You must miss your wife," I said.

"I do. Why are you not married?"

That was a subject that rankled me. "I have a boyfriend in the States, but, apparently, he has no desire to make space for me in his life. It hurt me so much that maybe that is the reason I came here."

"Do you want to get married?"

"It's not that important, but I want, like all of us, to be wanted."

"Yes."

Another English answer.

"You know," I said, "I think I am frightened of getting older alone. But looking at you, you dispel that. I thank you. I think my fear wanted my boyfriend to step in and assure me he would be there, and we would make our last years special together—"

"Well actually, he should. It's not an unreasonable request."

"Not unreasonable," I said, "but perhaps unrealistic."

"What do you mean?" he asked.

"It's probably not someone else's job to assure my last years are special. It is my job."

Now this conversation, understandably, was making him uncomfortable. We hardly knew each other.

"Let's talk about something else," I said, and he visibly brightened.

We chatted, and it was pleasant. And when we said good night, he surprised me by saying, "I think you're about to come out of hiding."

"It feels more like I'm going into it, living here."

"Doesn't matter where you are. Well, good night then, and we must do this again."

I reached up and kissed the Roman senator's cheek. He smiled. I was glad to leave, and I was glad I had come. Both parts had meaning.

Chapter Twenty-Five

I must call Lucia. I had left her a muffin as a joke since she always leaves me one. Of course, mine was left outside her door. Maybe an animal ate it by the time I had walked back to my place, even though I covered the muffin up quite well, but still, those animals are clever. I didn't know why I didn't call her. Today was a Jewish holiday so I wouldn't. Perhaps tomorrow.

When I got home to my little burrow, an animal myself, really, I opened my email and one of those "ideas" that had been bandied about for some time looked like it was coming real. Six books of mine in a collection. Now there was the interesting idea of, since I am unknown, who would want to read six books of mine in the first place or who would be the least bit interested, but this was not daunting the publisher, who lives in Paris, since she believes in them so. I had thought the whole idea fantastical when she came up with it. I knew I had always been on the outside, my books printed out of the mainstream, but still it was a little overwhelming. Joyce and Miller probably thought the initial Parisian publications of their books fantastical, not that I am in their league, I am speaking of the subject of the fantastical here, yet it was not absolutely fantastical since traditionally those who are nomads, literally or intellectually, have been published in France. The books will be in English. Talk about a mixed-up plan but, still, a body of work. To see a body of work as a little family of six, not that they were a series. Although, as with all writers, there is a continuous theme. Maybe not all writers. Whatever one says about writers can be disproven in the next sentence.

What she had sent me were marketing materials with quotes from my books. She sent me a podcast where she read lines from my books and I was astounded I wrote those lines, the first books so many years ago.

What I am trying to say is that whether it really happened or not, and it was looking possible, it made me feel real to myself. Oh, I have been doing something, and these are not even all my books and I saw such focus and dedication. Usually, I thought of myself as wasting time. The books revealed a person to me, in other words, I didn't mind being. This, in itself, was shocking and I knew was going to be transforming. It couldn't be anything but.

Now I was in the difficult situation of hoping for it, because it was only natural, a writer wants to see her books in book form with the hope of being read, a writer wants to talk to you, but I also had to not hope because it very well could not happen. She was in the business of raising money and so is everyone else in the world.

I had to go back to my childhood and adulthood stance of expecting the worst. Yet she, God bless her, was not like my mother who'd left me, she had a vision for me, a big one, one that was loving and giving, and she was putting her all, her money and her time, into it. After all, who puts out six books of an unknown author? An audacious vision, and that was what made me hope it would work because audaciousness, as in how Churchill had insisted upon fighting against all odds, should be rewarded. I wanted her to be rewarded for this incredible act of kindness and belief.

If she managed to succeed and get these books out, then all those young girl walks of mine, at fifteen, seeing a future of avant garde books, were not just wispy dreams but prescient. True, I was quite old for this, but I suppose that is when a collection comes out.

If she did pull this off, I would have had my children.

The days and weeks followed, and more messages came in. They were all set to print. A French translator had been secured. Titles were agreed upon (with me). The covers done, not to my great happiness but that is a rare event for any writer, the back copy written, the quotes chosen, the blurbs requested. She was serious.

I felt like an expectant mouse.

I listened to myself on a podcast interviewed about the collection and thought, Who are these women? What are they saying?

Some of those books, three of them, had been put in my drawer in shame. They are too full of pain, I thought.

"Let me decide," she'd said. "I want to read them." And she did and took notes. She kept affirming them, and then took them in.

It felt, just like Sir Leo had said, like I was coming out of hiding.

Chapter Twenty-Six

Skene popped by around 6:30, just about the hour when I couldn't stand any more discussion with myself about the meaning of this collection. I liked Skene's way of communicating. It was more intimate than email. "Drink?" he asked, at the door.

I grabbed my jacket.

The pub was very busy. People crowded in hallways having their pints, and at tables, and people carrying drinks navigated through to get to those tables. Skene got us a corner booth as if it were waiting for him.

He was said hello to and, what was even more interesting, I was also said hello to. "Hi Yank," which I did not like since I am at war right now with America. Never before in America did I get emails suggesting I download some app that would encrypt anything I wrote because the person who sent it seems to believe a major repression is coming.

I didn't want to believe it and when I communicate with my liberal friends, they think it is all hog wash.

"Yank," I said to Skene. "I used to sort of be proud of it. It felt free."

"Your president seems a nice guy," he replied.

"Most likely he is. But many think he is just another politician blowing the way the wind blows. And there are a whole lot of people coming out of the woodwork on my email who are concerned about the lack of truth being reported or even investigated. Instead, the media's political agenda is being reported, not the news. Nobody is digging deep if it means being independent in what you reveal and that, in itself, is so sad. And most people I know feel they cannot speak to friends about their political ideas unless they fall in with the prevailing party. They feel they are being silenced, in other words."

"Are they?"

"I don't know enough to know what is true and not true and God knows I am suggestible and enjoy being out of the mainstream so if everyone thinks the president is a nice guy, you can rely on the fact I won't, or if they think the president is tyrannical, I won't think that, either. It's all so confusing. Am I seeing reality or am I just being contrary? Are they?"

"Well—"

"I get all these emails from political fundraisers written in the language of 'we must get this or that person out of or into jail, and, if we don't, terrible things will happen.' All this fury and hatred. It feels a bit like a digital French Revolution."

He laughed.

"A colonization is coming, strangely and furiously, with all this groupthink, and I have a nature designed to hate colonization," I continued.

I smiled at him, and added, "I am a woman, after all."

He looked at me strangely. What are we talking about, he was wondering.

"I guess I distrust the party that paints themselves as righteous. But then, they both do."

"This is all because someone called you Yank?" he asked, laughing. He reminded me then of my ex-husband who hated a long answer to any question he asked me.

"I keep thinking I should reinstate my other two passports. Canada where I grew up and England where I was born. Let me add, in other ways, some of what is going on is wonderful. The opportunities for the poor. It is the media I hate."

Skene and I sat in silence as if we had this kind of conversation all the time. "You know," he said, "Matisse said it is very difficult to understand and appreciate the generation that follows you."

"Yes," I said. "Turns out to be true. What about you?" I asked. "How are things in your life? Makes for more upbeat conversation."

"I was thinking," he said, "that I might invite you to come look at some paintings with me. I am thinking of buying them or, minimally, looking at them."

"Oh, that would be nice, I might see more of the countryside."

"Well, they're not in the countryside."

"Where are they?"

"They're in Paris. I thought we might go to Paris together. Might be interesting."

"I see," I said.

"It's always fun to go to Paris," he said. "The food and the beauty and the museums. I like the Rodin Museum, among others."

"How would we get there?" I asked.

"I suppose the Chunnel."

That was great, too.

I smiled at him, raised my glass, and said, "I'm in."

"What's that mean?" he asked.

I thought for a minute. What does it mean? Had I just betrayed myself? "It means I'd love to go."

"Well, you can relax and celebrate that you're not completely mad, then," he said.

Some of the men in the pub began singing "The Way You Look Tonight" a cappella. Skene and I were both quiet listening, lost probably in our fear of doing a new thing with a new person. What if we couldn't stand each other?

I looked over at him and he was in a kind of reverie. What was he thinking about? A time in his life when he looked at a woman and she had looked the way she looked tonight, transporting. The song seemed to suggest that that is what a man wants. And I was thinking how it is highly unlikely I can look the way you look tonight at my age. Or maybe not, if I am happy, I guess. If I am happy, I might be able to.

George at the coffee shop has become a life guru without intending to be. When I first requested a coffee to go, he said, "You mean takeaway?"

"Yes."

"I don't have any of those paper cups."

"Oh."

"Why on earth can't you sit down for twenty minutes and enjoy a cup and my gorgeous face? What could possibly be so important that you have to race up the hill with a coffee like that? It's subhuman," he said, pouring me a coffee into a cup that looked almost like blue pottery. "You should slow down and enjoy things, for God's sake. Takeaway. Take away to where? You've got enough time alone, don't you, living up there in a hovel, like some old-time mystic. Except you dress like you come out of Paris, but really, sit down and relax and enjoy yourself. Give time to yourself. Let your mind go free. Stop. It's bloody important."

I sat down and looked out the window.

"Thank you, George."

"Yes, and anything else you need straightening out, you come here."

I laughed.

"Well, there is one thing," I said.

"What's that?"

"Where is Lucia?"

"Did you knock on the door another time?"
I felt a bit guilty about my answer so said nothing.
"Try that first, then we'll discuss it."

Chapter Twenty-Seven

I went home and did just that. No answer.

I scribbled on a receipt a note, "Just tell me you are okay. Your grateful tenant."

Twenty minutes later, I see her coming down the hill toward me, red hair flying, glasses falling on her chest, a big blue pullover with a colored scarf tied round her neck. In other words, European.

I opened the door and she said, "I heard you but I was too late getting to the door. I am sorry. A lot has been going on and I just have not been around too much. Are you hungry?"

"No, but I was worried."

"About what?"

"I haven't seen you at all. Going in or out."

"Oh, I am busy inside doing things. It doesn't mean anything."

"Well . . ."

"I am writing," she said, "what I am told to write."

"Told?"

"Yes. I don't often understand it, but I do it. It is important."

"I see," I said.

She laughed. "It is about the Bible. The female version."

"You are being told the female version of the Bible?"

I hesitated for a minute. "Did you start that after your second husband died?"

"That was when I began having visions, even while he was dying."

"Visions?" I thought of the dead fishermen in the water I had seen.

"I began getting messages," she clarified.

I was not sure what to ask next. She is receptive, I explained to myself. We should all be listening to our messages. She pays attention. She is open. Says yes. I thought all this in a millisecond as I filled up with love for her.

"Then I had dreams that were full of directives. In some ways, this has all kept me very lonely—"

"Like a mystic—" I said.

"Yes. But since I would not be happy just talking about what's for dinner, maybe I am meant for this," she added.

"Do you like being this alone?"

"I wish I was with someone. I believe it will come but it is in the future."

I believed her, too.

"I am busy," she continued, "writing, and I have children and grandchildren I see. They have their problems."

"I've never noticed them," I said.

"I go to them. They are not far away."

"Everybody has problems," I said.

"Yes." She looked at me. "But you, my dear, have a big soul."

"All of us do," I replied.

"I know what you mean, but I notice I have not had to explain anything to you."

"Alan Watts," I said, "wrote you need to be alone in the desert to find out who you are."

"So it seems," she replied. "But this is not the desert. We should go out for dinner and drinks some time," she added gaily. "We should enjoy ourselves."

"Good idea. But where?"

"There is only one place, but it is still fun. You know it."

"Okay, we'll do that." I smiled. "Let me know when."

She looked around the playhouse. "Everything all right here?"

"We need to get more heat."

"Yes, I will send somebody to put in some heaters."

"Thank you."

"Yes. See you later," she said, and off she went, purposefully, to transcribe or scribe a new Bible.

I forgot to mention to her that I am going away. I'll leave her a note. I forgot because I am a bit nervous about going. I am often uncomfortable with people if it is for a long period of time. I will stall Skene till I don't feel so nervous about it.

Meanwhile the publisher in Paris sends me final covers for the six books of mine. It astounds me, as astounded as Lucia is astounded at whatever is going on in her house.

I type to the publisher: *I am coming to see you.*

You're kidding." She thinks I am in the States.

No.

Hopefully we can celebrate the launch, she writes. *I feel so alive.*

Really? I replied.

Yes, I am surrounded by all this art, yours, these six covers, others' . . .

I realized that any creativity, any making of anything, is enlivening. I understood that the gallery owner, the collector, the house decorator, the carpenter get that electric jolt in fostering art, just as the artist does in making the work.

I know what you mean, I wrote. *Even if you can't launch, this whole thing has been almost life changing. That you believe in the books.*

A lot of forces are working with us, she wrote.

My hands hovered above the keys for my answer. I thought

about Skene saying, "Let's go to Paris." That was quite a coincidence.

I wrote her back, "You have no idea."

Chapter Twenty-Eight

I tried to write but I was beside myself in some way. Those titles all together. A lifetime of work. Books that I had hidden coming to life. It excited me, like a man you are in love with getting in touch. My real life had just got in touch.

I heard some kind of rustling outside, turned, and glimpsed a shadow disappearing. I didn't want to follow it.

After a while, I opened my door and there in front of me was a large bouquet of flowers, freshly picked, not from a flower shop. A ribbon round them, and they were in a blue and white vase. Which was very thoughtful given I didn't have a vase in this tiny house.

I took them inside.

I turned the vase completely around.

No note.

I didn't think for some reason it was Skene. I didn't think that was the kind of thing he did.

It must be the hundred-aire. He was gentlemanly that way. Skene, himself, was offering the flowers of Paris.

Chapter Twenty-Nine

"I'll have a car drive us into London—"

"All the way?"

"Why not?"

"Are you an art thief that you live so luxuriously?"

He looked nonplussed by what I'd said. Maybe I had offended him.

"So we take a car," I said evenly as a way of apology, rerouting us, so to speak.

"To St Pancras Station and then take the Chunnel—" he replied and went on to details. As I listened, I noticed we both had a smile we were trying to hide on our lips.

In the Chunnel, we read. I read Deleuze and he read about Joyce's wife. He looked a bit different, more urbane than he did at The Cavalier or his house. No cap and his dark hair was striking, it was odd for an older man not to have grey, although I could see some grey in his beard. He was wearing an expensive blue shirt, naturally, and a jacket.

I am partial to men who dress well. I was also a bit more dolled up with earrings and high heels, well, I wear them all the time anyway except during tennis, but a black skirt and a blue sweater with only one shoulder.

"I might buy something new in Paris. I mean, one should, shouldn't one?" I said.

"Probably."

Just what I needed, another expense. But how many times do I go to Paris?

"Also, I have a publisher there. I would like to see her, and her husband, too, I like him, he's an architect, but literary and they are marvelous people, and even, remarkably, incredibly happily married and—"

"Of course. Just pick a night and we can do it."

I thought she and I could talk business that night. I knew her husband wouldn't mind, and he's been a bit involved in some of her aesthetic decisions, helping to call the draw on her and my differences of opinion, strategizing about how to market differently to the French, the British, the Americans. Because his wife actually refers to sentences I have written when she speaks, something even I could not do since it would frighten me to attach to them like that, I thought Skene could learn who I really am by listening. I might find out who I am, too.

But more importantly I would learn more about him. So far, he had the bearing of a wealthy lighthouse keeper, solitary, a person who does not really need someone. Which was a bit of catnip for me. This is a man who will not try to change me since he himself wants to be left alone.

We four met at an Italian restaurant somewhat near where my friends live. We went downstairs and it was full of Parisians drinking and eating, with one couple not speaking at all, obviously married for many years. Irene, who is originally American, and JP were thrilled to see me with a man they could possibly approve of, since Skene, no matter what else, does not try to get all the attention, as Kurt did.

He was cheerful and wry with them, and Irene, who owns the press, was gorgeous with her flaming red hair and blue eyes and perfect body. She is the essence of charm, and her husband is tall, blonde, and also intelligent and always vivaciously interested in everything, and all of it felt like I had landed somewhere artistic, open, and possible. Why don't I live here? I thought. A question I ask myself everywhere I go. Maybe I can come here next.

Skene began talking about what paintings we were going to be looking at and JP, the husband, knew of them and they discussed some painters I had not heard of but that doesn't mean much since I don't really follow painters and then went on to discussing the town where Skene and I now live.

"If you come," Skene said, "you can stay with me and George."

"The dog," I clarified, so they did not think he was gay. "You can't stay with me," I added.

"No, she lives in a tall box."

"What do you work at?" JP asked Skene.

"I'm a doctor. But I mostly donate my time to clinics. Otherwise, I read, buy paintings, and I am supervising a house I am building on some of my land. A barn that one can live in."

That was interesting.

"What kind of doctor?" I asked. I had never done so before, which was a bit odd. I, who am usually so curious. But I also love to find things out indirectly. That is the way I trust them. Or maybe I just like the slant of it. That is the beauty of art. It is so very, very telling, indirectly.

"A GP, an anachronism," he said.

"That's so excellent," Irene said to him.

"I didn't know you were building a barn," I said.

"I designed it, and we'll see how it turns out. God knows."

He doesn't encourage talking about himself, I realized. Why? I wondered.

Irene then turned to me and asked quietly, "What made you go off like this? You never even mentioned it."

"I don't know. I felt like I was just turning around and around myself. Like a child going in a circle. So, to make the circle bigger, I decided to do something completely different."

Skene was listening, as usual.

Irene said, "Someone in a blurb for one of the books wrote your main character was on a quest for true love and happiness."

I scrunched up my face. "Whomever wrote that is a lousy writer or is wishing me ill."

JP laughed. "She may be right," he said of me.

"Maybe I was just saddened by things," I said, "and wanted to go somewhere and grieve."

"Sad about what?" Irene asked.

Skene piped up. "Maybe your heart got broken," he said.

"Exactly," I said, although I thought he was talking about himself.

"By whom?" Irene asked.

"By everything. By how nasty everyone is when I open the news, nasty statements spoken while going on about how much good they are doing for people. It's hard to believe they are doing any good with all this outrage. How people execute people figuratively—"

"That has always gone on," Skene said.

"And even literally. All these shootings in the States. There is some kind of rush to judge everyone, which feels more dangerous than it appears. I don't know." I was silent for a second. "Maybe I just left because I like to be alone more than I think."

JP and Irene looked at each other. They didn't seem alone. I looked at Skene. He was alone. I was alone. Yet it was that very aloneness that was pulling us together.

"I am, as you can well see," I said, "totally confused. I need to figure it out."

Disconcertingly, they all nodded in agreement, as if they themselves had figured it all out.

Chapter Thirty

We were staying at the Hotel Meurice. He had got us two separate rooms, which I thought the height of sensitivity. If he had not done so, I would have been annoyed at his presumption. That he had done so made me a bit sad we were not in one room.

Somehow, I had the feeling he knew that. It takes a long rope to lasso me, if indeed he was trying. I had no idea. I would say yes by the way he looked at me. And, also, I liked the way he complimented me.

We had been walking to meet Irene and JP, and men had looked at me on the street and Skene said, "These men seem to surveille you."

"Well, they like me because I appear independent," I explained.

"I don't think so," he'd said. "I think it's because of your long neck."

Just to be contrary as usual, I said, "You never see men in books going on about women because of their necks. They go on about other anatomy."

He was smart enough not to respond.

After dinner with JP and Irene, we had a drink in the bar. He crossed his long legs, and we were silent. Maybe that was also a good idea on his part. Maybe he was frightened I would volley with deflection, which would not have been wrong on his part and becomes, let's admit it, dull. Being silent leaves doors open and true, and maybe that was why I was in search of them. The hotel was playing music. A Sibelius violin concerto. That would never happen in the States. It was reason enough to move to Paris. We continued in silence. It was his preferred way, and, for me, it furthered the idea that I was on a retreat.

My phone rang. I didn't recognize the number, but still answered it. Telemarketing. Lisa with the Warranty Department for a car I don't own. Click.

People look so lovely here, I thought as I looked around. A blonde woman with a perfect face. Should I move here?

Skene watched all this activity in my mind by not looking at me directly.

I realized I wanted to touch his body. I didn't know how to, and I did not want to frighten him; all I knew was that my compass was flickering toward him.

I looked at him and thought, as he had probably thought, all things in good time. I will wait. He will wait.

Till we understand.

Anyway, there is something wonderful in waiting. It calls upon the better parts of ourselves. It shows a respect for value and a fidelity of spirit. It shows courage. It shows trust in the future. It shows belief that what is to come will come if it is meant to, even all appearances to the contrary. It shows that appearances don't mean a hell of a lot. It shows one believes in some undercurrent that is far stronger than the surface. It shows that you trust your fate.

"Do you think," he asked finally, "that she'll put all those books of yours out?"

"For some reason, I do."

"A body of work. Must be a bit shocking for you."

"Well, I will be shocked if it happens."

"Do you think it will?"

"I am waiting. I am in the very busy activity of waiting."

Chapter Thirty-One

Skene and I walked round looking at the paintings, but my idea of going to a gallery is where I find one painting with which I fall in love. I don't leave it but, as if I am an X-ray machine, take it into my veins. But I couldn't find a painting here that I took to enough, and that agitated me. I am not a voyeur type, I like to go inside something. I didn't understand what we were doing there. He didn't seem that interested in these either.

"Let's go upstairs," he said.

We went up a circular staircase, more security guards, to the top floor. As I followed him, I thought his long legs were the most beautiful piece of art in the place, and then we got upstairs where there was other work.

Some pretty French woman began bowing and scraping to Skene. "Ah, bonjour, Monsieur Skene, so good to see you again. I have some special pictures for you. Some champagne?"

And then a security guard brought out two painted black and gold chairs for us.

We sat down, and he crossed his beautiful long legs in his dark blue trousers. Moose have long legs like this, I thought. They fall in love for life. I watched him and he was very inside himself.

They brought us champagne, which I didn't really want but then, when I sipped it, was an unusually good champagne.

Then they brought out a painting for him and put it on an easel in front of him.

It was by a Greek painter living in London, all blues, the colors of the sea, with some white and touches of red, an abstract but with the sea rolling.

"Get it," I said. Or I would get it, I thought, although I was pretty sure in this type of place, I could not afford it.

He looked at me. "Don't you think we should see others?"

"Yes, of course."

I doubted very much any of them would have this ocean and heaven and sun mix, without that probably even being the painter's intention.

The next one was a watercolor nude. Also quite beautiful. Like all great art, that wonderful blend of what is in and what is not in just as important.

I wanted to say "Get it, too," but that seemed a bit bizarre.

"What do you think?" he said.

"I like it."

"Yes."

Out came another one. A good painting of a harbor with fishing boats, but not as original.

I didn't need to say anything. I could see in his face when he just nodded, as if to say move on.

Now a big one, but, even so, it fit on the easel. "North China Sea," the woman said softly.

It was also an abstract, with pastel colors, well balanced but not like that sea where the paint felt like the waves.

I could tell he agreed. As usual, I could tell without words.

Soon we left with the blue one that the painter had not titled. I always admire humility.

Chapter Thirty-Two

That night we had dinner alone. A lovely place near the hotel and of course the food was sublime, and I have never cared that much about food, but if you live in Paris, I could see one would care about food.

"Worth the trip, wasn't it?" he said.

"Yes, in every way."

He poured me some wine and I noticed that the waiter didn't do it and I thought this must be some sexual language the French understand. Because it was sexy having him pour the wine and not the waiter. Again, he was caring for me. It moved me.

"Are you going to buy the dress you wanted?"

"No," I said. "I don't really like shopping, and one doesn't need it in Lucia's box."

He nodded.

He studied me.

"What are you thinking when you look at me like that?" I asked.

"I don't know," he said. And something about the non-response of that warned me, perhaps correctly, perhaps incorrectly, that he might be even more withholding than Kurt. Kurt probably would have answered with something aggressive, something vaguely disappointing, not to mention Kurt didn't look at me much anyway, but whatever he did or did not do would have had the courage of his assurance.

Skene's response frightened me that he would not risk. I had my own problems in that area, I didn't need the same in another.

Chapter Thirty-Three

So it was not perhaps surprising that I woke missing Kurt. I felt I would like to have been with him in this hotel in Paris. I used to love our intimacy in hotels. We were always close, walking together through lobbies, through side streets, through breakfast rooms. Just close. I remembered spending Valentine's with him in New York. Coming in from tennis to meet him for dinner, and he would be waiting for me at a restaurant, sitting there in a green velvet jacket and silk shirt and we would have a wonderful dinner and just be together. He would lecture me on my tennis deficiencies and other matters but then he pulled out a sweet card and a picture of an emerald ring he'd bought me. "It's being sized," he'd said, and indeed it was exquisite when it arrived. He was not the type to buy people's hearts and we had been together for years when he did this, so it was moving to me.

That same Valentine's evening Kurt had sat me in his massaging chair since my back hurt, then on a heating pad he set up on the bed while I was in the massaging chair and then onto red light therapy that he swore worked. I did feel better in the morning. But mostly I loved how we entangled our legs and arms in bed. How I loved to touch his chest. We didn't do that at all at first when I met him. He used to insist on not touching, but I waited it out. As maybe he was waiting me out now.

I had fallen in love with Kurt immediately, and he had pushed initially that depth of feeling away and his aggressiveness in doing that was almost a pain I could not recover from. Skene is not like that, he does not proffer pain as part of our coupling, maybe a touch of indolence, but, even so, he already acts as if we are a pair, though we are not. I had joined myself to Kurt's body the second night I was with him, maybe I am drawn to pain, and that is what I am running from. How many reasons can one person have for leaving somewhere or someone?

I have not had sex with Skene.

As always, my mind traversing.

With one and wanting to travel back to the other. A worn route for me.

I could accept that about me, or I could fight it, or I could study it. Accepting it seemed lonely, fighting it seemed a waste of time.

I could probe for the truth. I could ask Kurt to come see me when I got back.

The French publisher was having trouble getting the money for the books. Well, she had only just started. I must stay out of it.

I went downstairs, and Skene and I had breakfast. Fruit and coffees for me. So pleasant to sit in a white dining room with white napkins and waiters in white jackets. Skene kept glancing longingly down at the newspapers that the maître d' had placed on our table. I said, "Go ahead and read them. I will, too."

Which he jumped to.

I had an interview on Zoom for a friend's article on aging that morning. I excused myself and went up to my room, logged on, and it was good to see my old friend with his inimitable humor. He said, "Okay if we wing it?"

"Of course."

"Where are you?" he asked on the screen.

"In a hotel room in Paris."

"Really? Why?"

"Came to look at some paintings with a friend."

"Do you feel old or young?" he asked.

"Young. When I was young, I felt old."

I felt, as I talked to him, that age was a joke life plays on us. At the end of the interview, he said, "Any advice on aging?"

"Yes, you should interview Sir Leo."

"Who is he?"

"A man who is one hundred whom I met playing tennis."

"Wow. Can you put us in touch?"

"Yes."

"Any other words of wisdom?"

"Love what you do. Oh . . . and who you're with."

I took the elevator back down to the breakfast room. Now if I could only follow my own advice.

Chapter Thirty-Four

We were alone in our compartment on the Eurostar back, Skene sitting next to his painting. He woke me from my reverie of just staring at the sight of movement itself out the window by saying, "Do you think I am in conjunction to the world?"

I looked at him, astounded. "What brought that up?" I asked. "You do know that 'being in conjunction to the world' is James Dickey's expression?"

"I can't remember," he said. I was surprised again he did not ask me who James Dickey is. "I asked," he continued, "because you seem to almost treat me as if I belong to another world."

I looked out the window and thought, I do, I do almost treat him as if he is of another world. But he does belong to another world than mine. And because he hardly ever speaks of this world or his world or the world that I have known, it puts him in another world. The silences between us create another world.

"Maybe I do treat you as if you're in another world. But I think of you"—I hesitated—"as in conjunction to an internal world." I was quiet for a second, then added, "Which I admire."

"Sir Leo? What about him?"

"I think he actually works with the outside world somehow. And internal. He has even picked up speed, I think, in connecting with the world since it is for him near the end of the race. The way he responded to me had speed to it."

"And I do not?"

Finally, finally, Skene is playing some cards.

"You are like me," I said. "I think you make a lot of time for your fears."

"I don't know," he said. "In truth, I have very few fears."

"That's probably true, too. But you do seem a bit fearful of relationships. Not that I can talk, but perhaps that is how I can tell." We were silent a bit, and then I said, "I wonder what we should do."

"Probably study. The fishermen."

I jerked my head up. "In the water?"

"Yes." Then, as usual, he picked up his newspaper.

"Well, what is it with the fishermen?" I quickly asked to get his attention. "That we both speak of them? Was I imagining something that once did happen? Are they ghosts? Who are they?"

"Oh, I don't think they really existed, do you?"

"But you just mentioned them."

"Doesn't mean they exist. You see fears in me that I don't see. I see needs and things in you that you don't see."

"You're saying we both are referring to something that we both have so-called seen that is not real?"

"Yes," he said. "Just like I could say people think they have heard or have seen God, like Lucia does," and then he snapped his newspaper so it was fully extended for him to read, and I could see we were back to mining silence.

I sat there a bit confused. What on earth are we talking about? No wonder he prefers silence. Which one of us is mad?

"Are the fishermen in the unconscious of many people here?" I asked.

"No," he said, "but if anyone is half awake, we all have to see them."

True, I thought. He himself was there that day I saw them. That day neither of us spoke. Is this some kind of revelation born of shared silence?

I pursed my lips and looked at the back of his newspaper. Well, this would reveal itself.

Chapter Thirty-Five

Kurt said he wanted to come visit. This was a bit surprising since he hates to go to any effort, and this would be a transatlantic flight and then a bit of a drive in a car. Maybe he needs an adventure himself.

I went round town looking for a hotel since my place is undoubtedly not up to snuff.

"George," I said, in the coffee shop, "someone is visiting, and is there a hotel here?"

George sat down at that, next to the counter. "Not really *in* this town. A few towns over."

"I need something here."

"Well, one of us can put him up."

"He might not mind that if the place is luxurious."

"What about your pal, Sir Leo? Does he have a cottage up there?"

"It doesn't seem right to ask him. He's not interested in making a few extra dollars."

"No," he said. "Let me think and ask around. I'll tell you tomorrow."

"Okay. Keep elegant and luxury in mind. Not where I am."

"Got it. What is he? A prince or something?"

"In his own mind, yes," I said.

"Well, aren't we all," he said, as he wiped his hands on his apron.

"I agree," I said, and turned toward the door and was almost outside.

"What about asking Skene?" he yelled out.

"Very funny."

George found a place owned by Mrs. Shapiro. "She's an odd sort," he said. "A beautiful place with a turret over the sea. Had the best decorators, all that in from London. She adopts these children who come through. Some of them difficult, but she does it."

"Impressive."

"More coffee? Of course, more coffee." He poured. "Yes, a handful. Anyway, she has a cottage, with gorgeous windows and its own private place, and should be perfect for an American prince."

"Oh, thank you so much. Is it expensive?"

"She says she doesn't need the money. These orphans of hers will probably like to meet an American. One of them will eventually move there, let's face it."

I smiled.

"So, we're all set," he said, proudly.

"What would I do without you?" I asked.

"You did fine for quite a few years."

"Better now."

This kindness of his was the first healing. I actually left there practically dancing. I also was happy Kurt was coming. I had a long history with him. Maybe I would stay with him in that cottage and we would go somewhere new, farther out into the desert sandstorms and radiant sunsets of love. Of course, I would stay with him.

Kurt went directly to Mrs. Shapiro's once he arrived. He texted me where the place was and that the flight went well, and he was looking forward to seeing me and needed to take a quick nap and why don't I come over. Yes, I texted back. Be right there. I had never been to Mrs. Shapiro's, and, as I walked, I realized it was both exciting to see Kurt, someone close to me from another world at this point but my world, and also exciting to be seeing new terrain as I traveled. As I went toward her house, I saw she lived on a jutting piece of land over the beach and her house was high up. Quite beautiful. I went up the road toward it and the landscape was not tended at all, a bit askew. I worried that maybe Kurt's place was going to be the same.

But when I walked into the little cottage, it was neat and pretty with curtains and a double bed, and a window over the sea, but I hardly looked because, when I saw him, I was struck at his handsomeness, his essential maleness, the wiry grey hair, the strong nose, wide shoulders, and how he gave off a feeling of power. I was not sure what it was exactly about him. Clothes don't make the man as much as he likes to think; it was more in the way he held himself so straight and his mildly mocking way of looking at everything, which was both entrancing and off-putting. Maybe the confusion of that puts one on an unsteady level. A power move.

In other words, we immediately began teasing and playing, and we were quite happy together and I joined him for a nap and all the ensuing sedatives between a man and woman before sleep.

He was happy to be here and struck by the beauty of the island, and I once again got the feeling he badly needed a change of scene himself.

I could tell by what he said: he had seen no dead fishermen.

That was perhaps his good luck or not.

He told me news of his grandson, his son's and his own business, news of how crazy his chef was. This was all old news but still good to hear his particular sentence structures.

"There is only one local here, and I will bring you for dinner," I said. "The people are lovely."

"How is the food?"

"I don't know, but this is not an epicurean trip you're on."

He laughed.

In essence, we were both happy to be together and why was I running away from him, I asked myself.

He looked at me cheerfully and I smiled back, and I could see a sort of purring inside him that I was still enthralled with him and all I had done was just go off.

Chapter Thirty-Six

It was a wonderful evening at The Cavalier where Kurt seemed to enjoy the people coming up and saying hello and introducing themselves and asking, "Is it really true?" about the politics in America. He likes to pontificate and there was ample opportunity. We walked home under a starry sky, and, for a New Yorker, that is as novel as seeing the aurora borealis, since the tall lit buildings obfuscate any light in the Manhattan sky. The next morning, he wanted to see where I lived.

We walked over to my dollhouse, and I know he is not that fond of walking but he seemed to enjoy just the quiet, as I had.

When he saw my little box, he was a bit shocked at how small it was and kept remarking that he couldn't see how I could stand it. Then I saw, most unusually, Lucia walking down the hill toward us.

I opened my door to her.

"This is Lucia, my landlord. I told you about her."

Lucia smiled at him, giving him a beautiful smile, and I thought she must have launched a few thousands ships in her time.

He rose to the occasion and channeled his inner shipping magnate.

"Don't you miss her?" she asked him, referring to me.

"Of course. That is why I am here."

"But why is she here? I am happy she is, but why did she come, do you think?"

Kurt never liked these kinds of questions. He likes things to be on the surface, but he tried to be polite. "These creative types like to move about."

"I think she is looking for something she could not find back home. Or maybe running from it," she said.

"She has a pretty nice life back home," he said. "I think it is just an adventure."

"Something is bothering her," Lucia said.

"Something is bothering all of us," he replied.

She looked at him and said, "Well, whatever it is, it will come out." She smiled at him and said, "I take it you are not staying here. It's probably too small, I understand. Anyway"—she turned now—"I hope you enjoy your stay on our island."

"Yes," he said, "what is there to do here?"

"Do?" she asked, turning to us.

"Yes, anything to see? Do?"

She thought. "I think what there is to do is just be. You'd be amazed how much goes on."

I smiled, and off she went.

A phrase went through my mind, and I was not sure who wrote it. Somehow it felt like Nietzsche, but it also sounded too colloquial for him. *Beware of the superficial.*

"Let's go for a walk," I said. "I will show you the harbor."

You can DO a seal while you're there, I thought.

We went down the hill and there is a lovely park by the water, and we began to walk through it and along its paths, some boats going by, even a cargo boat, and suddenly we were part of a funeral party. I recognized some of the people from The Cavalier. They nodded to me, and I saw Mrs. Shapiro, whom I had met by now, all in black as one of the walkers and she saw me and stepped back and said, "Hello, we are going back to my house after if you two want to come for lunch and some cocktails."

"May I ask who died?"

I had a terrible feeling it might be Sir Leo, but it didn't seem like it.

"Oh," she said, "he was an elderly man, a decent sort but his time had come, dear."

Kurt looked a bit uncomfortable but very vibrant against all these people in black walking slowly. He looked like someone who had places to go. He looked powerful, urbane, sophisticated, and a captain of industry. Perhaps it was the expense of his clothes, his straight bearing, his shrewd eyes on a handsome face.

"What do you think?" I asked him.

"Well, we have to go home anyway. I can take a nap after a nice lunch at their place."

"I can see you're very sentimental about the dead," I joked.

Inside Mrs. Shapiro's house, which was furnished expensively and tastefully with many rooms, Kurt whispered, "I wonder where she gets her money."

I ignored the comment. Everyone sat around politely chatting. The widow who lived near me was there and I introduced her to Kurt. The older avuncular uncle and his girlfriend, Penelope. They chatted with him a bit about "What is really going on in America" and Kurt was now bored with that subject and managed to make incomprehensible innuendos and not say anything serious.

I noticed suddenly that one of Mrs. Shapiro's girls, with hard eyes and almost a little girl's dress on a lean body, very young, was particularly fixated on Kurt. I could see he was exciting to her. After all, Kurt looked different than everyone there. Busier, more driven.

Kurt had me get him a drink and some food and finally he sat down in one of the big chairs that was almost a small couch. He began eating and the young woman came up to sit close to him and just stared at him. I was half watching them and half chatting with people. There was undoubtedly something lascivious about her, in counterpoint to her extreme youth. She had this bald hunger for whatever riches she ascribed to him.

I knew Kurt was drawn to very young women. I never quite understood why except for the obvious reasons. But was it the innocence of them or the adoration? Or the freshness?

This young woman did not seem innocent, but she must be since she was so young. She kicked her legs out and shot him very seductive and craven looks. He at first avoided them but then he was stirred by them. I suppose his mind conjured up all kinds of advantageous situations.

I watched slightly, not wanting to, but my mind understood all the subtexts and I watched and did nothing to stop it because I did not want to ruin Kurt's opportunity. Or maybe I liked hurting myself or I did not know how to protect myself. Or maybe I wanted to be the girl. Maybe I thought I could learn something from the girl. Maybe she was expressing my own wanton desire. She was so confident of her prey, and he was now so confident of his.

They began talking. I could not hear what they were saying. I couldn't imagine what they were saying. Whatever it was, I thought they would be subliminally negotiating.

Suddenly I saw Sir Leo. He was standing at a window, politely listening to someone and laughing.

I went up to him.

"Hello, dear," he said. "Have you been playing tennis?"

"Yes, and why can't I simply go after every ball? A dog would do better at it."

"Well," he said, "for one thing, you're not a dog."

I looked at him. "Did you leave me flowers?"

"I did. You were so sweet the night you came over."

"I was?"

"Yes. You manage somehow to connect with a person. I think just by being honest. You must come over again for dinner."

"I will. I'll return the vase, and once again thank you for bringing me the flowers. It was such a treat."

"Come next Saturday."

Kurt will have left, I thought. "Delighted," I said.

I went to look for Kurt and suggest maybe we go play tennis since that is one of his passions also. He had brought his racquet, I noticed.

I said "Excuse me" as I walked through people, only to see his chair was empty, and the girl was gone, too.

I looked around. My heart sank. Could he really?

I went upstairs looking for them, already feeling slightly sick.

"Do you know where the ladies' room is?" I asked.

"That way, dear."

The door was locked, and I put my ear to the door.

I know his sounds well. And there was no doubt in my mind what she was doing with him in the bathroom.

I went back down and poured myself a stiff drink. What on earth do I do now?

I could run to my hotbox. In fact, I would, and not see him at all. Let him and his acquisitiveness go.

Naturally he will deny it.

This is my moment about whether to trust myself.

I went back upstairs and knocked on the door.

Just as I heard him groaning in happiness.

You have your confirmation, I said to myself.

He will use some other excuse.

I put my ear to the door again.

And then I had it. I heard her giggle.

I knew this was not an incipient love affair, as I stormed to Lucia's playhouse. Even I would have trouble talking with that girl.

They are alike, I told myself. They are both hungry and opportunistic. For them, that is what one does. She saw it and liked it in him. You buy low and sell high. You talk down the price. You pride yourself on what you take from someone else.

I opened my door. Climbed the ladder, lay down, looked out at the sea, and cried.

Chapter Thirty-Seven

Of course, he texted me. *You are crazy,* he wrote. He got angrier and angrier in his texts. Hadn't he come all the way over here? *Why do you imagine so many things? What is wrong with you?* Then the texts just became *YOU ARE WRONG.*

I didn't answer any of them.

An email came in from a friend who had decided to support the books in France. Kindness, oh, I needed kindness now.

I stayed in my hut.

Lucia, in her inimitable way, brought food every now and then and didn't say a word. I knew and she knew she had seen it in him.

But I am an active person and not the type to lie about. Like all of us, I know movement heals wounds.

I dragged myself to George's.

"You look bloody awful," he said to me as he gave me a coffee.

"Again? It seems you're always saying that. It's not good for my self-esteem, George."

"What the hell happened to you?"

"You don't want to know."

"All right," he answered. A woman would have said, "No, tell me. I want to know. Maybe I can help." George, being a man, took me at my word. I appreciated it.

I sat there thinking. I almost wanted to see the dead fishermen. Maybe they would have the answer about what I should do next.

I didn't want to see Skene. I didn't want to see anyone. I just felt gapingly wounded. An animal skulking around with internal bleeding.

I walked down to the sea and sat down. I imagined that Kurt was in a car to the airport back to the States. Maybe he has taken that girl with him as some perversion of punishment and sexual feeding.

Look, you are old, I told myself. Maybe you should give all this up. But it is life we are talking about. I am not giving it up.

Maybe now I could move to Paris. Maybe God, as Lucia would say, has set the coast free for me to begin a new real life, a full-time one. Kurt was the anchor before that kept me tied to New York. Maybe now I could set sail in a new way. Maybe this whole place I was in now was to set a new direction.

But right now, I was still hurting so much I wasn't sure I could muster the energy to even get from George's coffee shop back to Lucia's hut, never mind Paris.

I stood up and trudged along to my box on the hill, as someone had called it. The answer would present itself.

It always does. And I must receive whatever comes.

Chapter Thirty-Eight

I have a strange nature. I can rarely stay angry at anyone since while I busily go over their transgressions, another part of my mind is also working on their defense.

So as I lay there in my bed over the sea mulling over Kurt's disrespect for me, there were also these sporadic rationalizations annoyingly breaking into my self-righteous grieving.

Hadn't I once had sex with a very young man surreptitiously (although everyone in that house seemed to know) as he went after me and his desire was so focused that it was the desire itself that was erotic because the event itself was absolutely uninteresting, if I recall. All this tension for a few seconds of unconsciousness. I suppose that is why it is called the little death. All this tension (life) resulting in a brief (or in the latter case, long) unconsciousness.

Of course, I didn't have a boyfriend in the same room, so it was not as egregious as Kurt. But I had been staying with a gay friend who was interested in that young man and that had not stopped me from inappropriately giving in to someone else's so-called desire.

In other words, is Kurt to blame for being human? For being weak? As if I am not?

My internal arguments went on and I know my juries. They rarely convict. The defense for everyone out there who has transgressed against me is my guilt about my own vagaries. Who am I to throw glass at glass houses?

That said, I had no intention of answering my phone if or when he got in contact. Yet I knew in time I would forgive him because part of my good health, I am sure, is that I don't hold on to anger.

But I do hold on to aloneness.

It was Saturday, my dinner with Sir Leo. He would be the first person I had seen for a week. One reason I was not canceling was that I was hungry. I just hadn't had the energy to ferret for food anywhere, and Lucia's occasional muffins or nuts weren't enough.

As I took the long walk, it was a beautiful evening again, and, just as before, it raised my spirits. I remembered I had been sad walking here the other time I came, and here I was, sad again. My loneliness for Kurt made me just want to sleep so I would not feel it. But instead, I was, as always, reading and writing and handling disparate emails and a request to write a ten-minute piece on gratitude that I accepted to force me not to be morose. I also had to come up with some clever marketing lines for something else I had written, and all this pushed me to carry on, but when I was finished with my work, back I went to lying down.

As I trudged along to Sir Leo's, I looked down at the emerald ring Kurt had given me and loved its elegance. I had loved his own elegance. He could come off as asynchronous, rude, even, and full of non sequiturs, but I just saw it as creative. And my soul needed that. The parts of Kurt that were creative and playful were the parts that were a match for me.

As I walked in the evening, I thought it so sad that he was not here seeing this beauty with me. But he had chosen cheap instant gratification rather than this soft, almost spiritual world here.

I was just rounding to the cypress trees in front of Sir Leo's mansion. Maybe he would have the answer without my asking the question.

As before, he opened the door before I knocked. I liked that.

He was welcoming and not pretending that he was not waiting for me. He must have been a good husband, I thought. Willing to show kindness.

"There you are," he said.

I nodded and handed him first the vase he'd left the flowers in and then I handed him an expensive wine I had bought in the town wine shop. I must say for a tiny hamlet, the wine shop almost outdid any in New York. But why was I surprised by that? As far as true culture was concerned, this place did not scrimp or try to pass off things as good that weren't. It had not one knickknack shop. No billboards. No phony signage promising outlandish things that insulted the readers' intelligence. How could it, with this natural beauty? It would be an insult to the green and yellow hills.

"Thank you," he said.

"Thank you," I said, "for inviting me."

There stood the silver tray with the vodka wearing its silver pendant. The silver ice bucket. The silver trolley standing against the window with the fulsome garden behind it, pale roses dotting the landscape. I watched him making the drinks and it reminded me a bit of Kurt and how he would often have cocktails ready when I arrived. I tried to return to the present.

"Well, how have you been?" I asked.

"Quiet. I've been reading an interesting book," he said, sitting down with his drink.

"About what?"

"It's called *The New Waw*."

My head jerked up.

"Yes, it's by a Tuereg nomad. Written in French. Beautiful writing. He wrote it in Paris, I think. Anyway, I don't understand what's going on in the book, but the writing has captured me."

"I know a bit about the Waw," I said. "I even thought this place was my Waw."

"What a coincidence," he said. "Is it?"

"I think I've realized everywhere is." I took a sip. "But the answer is yes."

"Makes sense," he said, crossing his legs. "I think I thought it was too, for me, and in some way it is, also—I mean, its physical beauty is breathtaking, and I don't ever walk without feeling almost lit by how exquisite it is and that I get the chance to see it. I do believe," he continued, "it is the secret of my longevity."

"How so?" Although I knew the answer. I had come here myself to get the deadening weight of all the rubbish out there off me.

"The perfection of this place renews my cells."

"Funny, I believe that my good health has something to do with not being angry," I said, just as I thought, Aren't I here on this island because I am angry?

"But you must be a bit angry to be alone like this," he said. "I mean, you're attractive. Why aren't you with a man?"

I didn't reply.

"You know, the nomads, one of the things about them," he went on, "is that they know how to get their needs met. They know where their sources are. There is a sort of intuitive network among them."

"Yes, I know," I said.

"Well," he said, standing up, "let's go have dinner. Maria has to get back home, so let's have her serve and then she can take off to her family."

"Of course, thank you."

"You're surprisingly quiet tonight," he said.

"Sometimes it's good to listen."

"I could not agree more."

When he said that, I began to feel a bit cheerier, lighter. I obviously needed that boost of confidence. Someone agreeing with me.

We sat down at the dining room table, which looked lovely with its candles and the old silver, and I wondered how Maria felt about polishing it all. Maybe it was a Zen activity for her. Where did people have to run off to here, anyway?

"After dinner I must play for you some Erik Satie I've been learning," he said.

"Oh, how lovely. What piece?"

"Gnossienes No. 4, 5, and 6."

"You teach yourself?" I asked.

"Well, I know how to play, so I learn new pieces. It was quite an ordeal getting my piano here. I had to have it delivered in pieces and then put back together."

"You must have a piano tuner?" I asked.

"Yes, a man a few villages away."

"He is one of your sources, then?" I asked.

He laughed. "You're absolutely right. Not the piano tuner, but the music."

Maybe I should marry the piano tuner, I thought, and disappear. Never leave his cottage.

"I too play the piano, a little bit," I said. "I have played those Satie pieces. Of course, not well, but they are very pleasurable to finger and listen to."

"How long have you played?"

"A bit all my life, but I am itinerant. Take it up and then drop it since it is not my primary art. I am lazy about practicing, and I have rarely found a good teacher to handle my flaws. But I too am a music addict, just sadly not a musician."

He took this in and then asked, "So how has your week been?"

"A little up and down. I had a friend come from the States, and we did not part on good terms."

"Terrible," he said. "I am so sorry."

"Yes. There are downsides to being an older woman."

"I don't think of you as such. And anyway, you'll find there are advantages to aging."

"Oh? What do you find them to be?"

"Well, if I was a younger man, you would be playing a cat and mouse game with me right now about will we get involved or not, but instead we are having a very enjoyable evening and can just be friends with no agenda."

"And is that better?"

"It's not as much game theory, so to speak, but there's more trust, maybe. You think I can't hurt you."

"I'm sure you can if you want to."

"I can't be integral to you because of my age."

"I am not sure I agree."

"Well, time will prove us out."

I looked at him oddly and didn't want to ask what he meant.

"I wonder how I can help you," he said.

"What do you mean?"

"I don't know. I don't even know why I want to."

"You're a very peculiar lord, or whatever you are," I said. And I smiled, simply enjoying his tall straight elegance, his strong, dark, intelligent eyes, his command. But I also enjoyed how he nomadically traveled around different conversations.

"Oh, I think we all are peculiar, in point of fact. Do you think you'll make it up with your friend?"

"No, I don't," I said.

"Why not?"

"He was too willing to hurt me."

"Hurt passes."

"But I would never trust him, and that's a lonely life."

"You already have a lonely life," he said, and as he said it, I could hear Maria yell out from the kitchen, "I'm finished clearing up. See you tomorrow."

"Lovely, thank you," he called back.

But I didn't want to lose our conversation. "I do have a lonely life, but this lonely life could change. But if I stay with him, it won't. He will hurt me again."

"How do you know?"

"He showed his nature."

"I see."

"I'm glad you do because I am not sure that I do, but I know that we should be kind to each other. That's all I know, and he was not kind to me."

"Yes." And here I lost Sir Leo to his own thoughts. Finally, he said, "Why don't you come and play the piano here sometimes. I could teach you some pieces. It will do you good."

I thought a bit. I did like playing the piano, although, as mentioned, I play the piano like I play tennis, never excelling. But I did like the trying. I liked not giving up. As if I was making up for something in the past. Someplace where I had gone off the rails by pushing away any desire for myself, and this present attempting, this present desiring, to hit a ball or at times hit piano keys or a new place or meet a new person or take on a new piece of art that I myself was making, it was as if they were all thin funnels toward something new and vibrant, away from the time when I had not been willing to try. I had been so hurt when young by those nomad parents who seemed to love and value movement more than the caring for me.

"What do you think?" he asked.

I was wondering what he meant and then I remembered he was talking about my playing his piano.

"It would be great."

"We can make a plan," he said, with a very directive manner. "Let's say you come round every Thursday at 4 pm. I'll give you a lesson and then we'll have a cocktail, and you can return home."

"Were you a piano teacher?" I asked.

"Not at all. But we're not taking on the Appassionata. Just some gentle Chopin maybe, and I'll see what else."

He was very cheerful, I saw, at this moment, expansive, as if he was in charge of something.

"Music is my Waw," he said.

I ran into Lucia a few days later. "I am so glad," I said, "that you put that radio in."

"Are you feeling better?" she asked.

"Yes. I'm even going to take piano lessons from Sir Leo."

"Oh, that's funny," she said.

"Why? What's funny about it?"

"He was a conductor years back. You should look him up. Very good. These music people stay young," she said. "Have you noticed? A lot of them live on and on."

"I never heard of him."

"How do you know? You don't believe Sir Leo is his real name, do you?"

"I did."

"I think he's from another country."

"Well, how do you know he was a conductor if Sir Leo is not his real name?" I asked.

"It's a feeling I have."

"Too much imagination," I laughed. "You're as bad as me." I did not mention the fishermen at that moment but thought I might eventually. I felt she would completely understand and know what it was I did see. She would have the answer.

She smiled. "Maybe," she said. "You and I have that in common. Our imagination leads us places. That is good," she added.

Chapter Thirty-Nine

I saw the man at the window again, by which I mean I saw someone, maybe that man or maybe another man, but someone was indeed following me. I could not say definitively the man I kept seeing on the street was the man I saw at the window that first night I was here, even though both have dark hair. This man was a bit plumper and shorter, yet I didn't really see the entirety of the person at the window that first night, just the intensity of the eyes, so who knows? After all, I had thought the man at the window was a dream. This one on the street was absolutely real, an odd man whom I'd espied previously at corners and skulking round houses, whom I felt could not speak English, or maybe not even speak.

When I walked to George's for breakfast, that man would be on one of the side streets watching me. If I went to tennis, he was on a different side street watching me. Something about him frightened me, although in truth, when I did look at him, he did not have a beard like the man at the window. And he never did anything strange except look at me.

But still, I felt I was being followed, and it unnerved me.

This went on for quite some time.

I didn't want to mention it to George at the coffee shop because I felt this was between this man and myself.

And then one day I was walking about a bit farther, exploring, and it was a warmer day and I'd found another little coffee place where I decided to sit by an open window and I put my head out so I could really feel the sun, and there he was outside the window looking at me directly.

I didn't know what to make of it.

And then he reached through to pass me something. I took it reluctantly and opened my hand to see what it was, and it was a glass heart.

And, instantly, all my anxiety melted away. I felt such tenderness for him. We smiled and I thanked him, and his smile showed he was happy that he had made me happy and then he turned around and left, and I was left caring for him.

But the really frightening part started afterward. As I walked back, I thought about Kurt and the way he touched me. If I went to put my arms around him, he would make noises like a gorilla and back away. If I reached to kiss him or put my arms around him, he would sort of tickle me or grab my vagina no matter where we were, which of course made me recoil. In bed, he would sometimes sort of play with my body like it was a toy and I would feel repulsed. And he knew it.

No wonder he was looking for someone else.

And no wonder I had moved away to recover from something I did not understand, which I now thought, similar to the tale of the skulking man with the glass heart, might be about not knowing how to feel safe with a man.

When I thought of these books in Paris coming out, if they were coming out, each book except the last told tales centering around a fear of being loved. And some men in the books treated "my character" horribly. And "I" treated some men horribly, too, when "I" felt "I" was being captured.

I and my female characters were not comfortable with men, I realized. In real life, I could mask it with charm and wit occasionally, but, in truth, I was on guard.

This was not normal.

I understood now that I had taken myself to somewhere of sublime natural beauty to heal. Of course, this fear of trusting would not be a reason I would give to anyone when I was asked repeatedly why I had made such a move. A reason I had not even, till now, given to myself.

As I walked back, fingering my glass heart, I thought, I have to try, I have to let someone touch me. Just a little bit at a time, and experiment at being safe.

I was not interested in what caused this. I am too old for that. Damaging love affairs? Childhood? Who cares? I was interested solely in becoming whole. It was more important than mining the why. Getting healthy would heal whatever wound had happened.

I didn't have a plan for this recovery, but at least I was sure I must recover.

Chapter Forty

I rene in Paris is focused and productive, almost relentless. It is impressive. Do I like the bio? Do I like the one-line descriptions of the stories? This and that. The best thing for me to do is give simple answers and not get in the way with my flair for holding things back. The day before, a former student wrote me, *The thing about your success is that you even exist.*

I knew this was an unconscious insult. The whole thing was dizzying, but of course life is always a paradox so why am I surprised that, on one hand, a woman is going to all this effort to bring me out, and on the other, someone is saying, How did you live as itinerantly and as so much of an outsider as you did and manage to survive?

But to keep your head when all about you are losing theirs. Or in my case, when they have theirs, and I feel like I am losing mine.

Meanwhile, naturally my money keeps dwindling down. I am not working as much here and then I am keeping up two places.

I always lived as if I had money even when I had none. In other words, I, unlike so many people, don't really believe in money. Money, to me, is like myself: transitory.

Yes, it can make many lives pleasant, but I always thought the way to outsmart that was to have a pleasant life anyway, not making it dependent on money.

Mostly I have accomplished that through the generosity of friends and my own willingness to work at anything and everything to keep afloat.

Working at anything and everything also happens to open tremendous doors of temporary interest and adventure, which makes one rich in experience, so, all in all, money to me is some sort of seeking of flow and the rest is kind of uninteresting. I admire those so-called poor people who put $1000 into bitcoin and manage to sustain themselves on their investment, but I wouldn't even know how to think about it. There is so much else more interesting to think about.

That reminded me to go to Sir Leo's for my piano lesson.

It amused me that no matter where I go to get away, I become busy. I went away in search of time where nothing pressed on me and I immediately self-sabotage through my own enthusiasms.

"Ready?" he said as he opened the door on the dot at 4 pm.

I also planned to find out a bit about his background.

"Good afternoon, Sir Leo," I said, and I did think I saw a bit of a smile cross his face.

"You may not need to be so formal," he said.

"What should I call you, then?"

"Tanek. It means the one who is immortal."

"Is this a joke or your name?"

"Freud and that man who wrote *The Unbearable Lightness of Being* understood that that question is irrelevant."

All right, I thought. "I see."

We sat down at the piano, which had pink and white roses on top of it. The same kind he had left outside my door.

There was a booklet of Shubert music on his piano.

"I may not be good enough for that," I said.

He sat himself down at the keyboard and began playing some Etudes Symphoniques.

As he played, I said, "Clearly you *are* good enough."

And then we both were transported to perfection as he was delicate at times, and precise, so precise, and other times staccato, not forcefully but gracefully.

"Dame Myra Hess played this," he said as his hands continued all over the keys, "with the Philharmonia Orchestra. You're too young to know who she is."

Then he focused on his playing, gaining in intensity. Enjoying himself thoroughly at his virtuosity.

I made a note to look up who were the conductors for the Philharmonia Orchestra.

He went on, the sun was out, the garden was alive, and now everything in life seemed wholly perfection and immeasurably exquisite.

He flourished at the end, and then turned to me, eyes smiling and still perhaps a bit inside the music.

"So," I said, "you are an artist."

"Dame Myra Hess played this so beautifully, much better than me, obviously. She performed in a way to learn from." He stood up.

"I am not even going to try that," I said.

"Oh yes, you are."

And then we spent an hour on the first chord. I finally got it, and it was fun, as were his stories about music that I got to take breaks with.

Maybe Lucia is right about him. But he did not want to say anything about himself, and I don't know, in this day when everybody is touting themselves no matter their lack of or abundance of talent, I couldn't think of anything more musical.

Then it was time for the silver tray, and he put on some Janacek.

"Idyll for String Orchestra," he said.

I looked out the window, and it seemed even the flowers were dancing.

"He started composing quite late, in his seventies, I think," Sir Leo said.

"I really want to keep calling you Sir Leo," I replied. "It's so amusing, even if you are immortal."

"By all means," he said, laughing.

He sat down and crossed his legs. I considered that a magical feat at his age, although, like all magicians, he made it look easy. I squinted at some medal on the wall. It was not prominently placed but in an unobtrusive corner.

I walked over; it was a medal indeed. Royal Philharmonic Orchestra 1939.

I sat back down.

"Knickknacks," he said.

"Not quite."

But I too was enjoying the lack of banal conversation that elderly people can sometimes get into of "I used to . . ."

Sir Leo or Tanek didn't bother with it. He was in the moment, one with the flowers outside and Janacek inside.

Chapter Forty-One

One of my brothers lives in Holland. He knows I am now physically closer to him, not being in the States, so he said, since he used to work in the airline business, he could fly over for nothing, and it would be an easy flight. He is retired and perhaps bored.

We have never been close, yet are not hostile in any way. We simply do not have much in common. He's had children, married, been a businessman, smart about money and marriage, moved everywhere, so much so that I thought he might be in the CIA, but I don't think he was. It was just he always seemed secretive. I think he had our parents in his blood, and since he did not like our parents, by proxy, he was guarded with me and a bit judgmental. I lived insecurely financially (like our father), theatrically (like our mother), had no children (like our mother who left us), did not settle with one person (like both our parents), and when he looked at me, he saw all of this made manifest. It made him nervous and resulted in his movements with me being slightly aggressive and pained.

When I looked at him, I too was made uncomfortable because I saw how our parents had hurt us in many ways by their insensitivity, and I saw it because he hid his sensitivity so acutely, and there was such sadness in his eyes, and anger in his voice, since neither of our parents had been particular caretakers although our father did try, better with me than my brother, and so when I saw the terrible feeling of injustice in my brother's face, I saw some of my own.

We were difficult for each other.

But also as you age, my mother—of all people—had said, "Family becomes more important," and in that she was right.

And the past, we know, never leaves and pops up in odd ways all the time. As the sun went down last night I had been thinking about Canada, where we grew up, and its plains, its oceans, sunsets as long as eternity, and its hopefulness in being a new country with not that many people, and I began to cry, longing for those majestic mountains and all that open space.

My brother arrived and I met him at the same dock where I myself had first landed. He is tall and good-looking and, as I said, nervous.

His opening words were, "I always told you: you should move somewhere like here. You don't have enough money to be anywhere else."

"Well, I haven't moved. I am just here to see what I feel."

"Get out of New York, it's so expensive, and just settle down."

I sighed. How men like to tell you what to do. "How are you?" I asked.

He went on to speak about his daughters, one who is accomplished and another doing it her own way, and he faintly blames our bloodline for the one who has difficulties. I, the poorest of us all, had invested in a small business for the one doing it her own way that went nowhere.

But I asked for it. I was trying to help and pushed my idea onto her. She is not driven and is a dreamer, although she has brains. Both girls do. So did my mother and me. But all of us women, all of us traveled and never stopped traveling solo in the desert.

My brother's girls have a nice mother, so they will fare better.

We walked around and I saw the man who had the glass

heart sitting on one of the turrets by George's coffee shop and I waved to him. He smiled with great joy, and that gave me hope to carry on.

My brother used to be a fool to me. Impaired, damaged, and so difficult that I thought he made all the wrong decisions, but then he became a minor captain of industry; he did all the right things and because of that he has a more solid life than I do. It became clear at one point it was me who was the fool, not him.

I used to treat him as if he needed my help. Now, he treats me as if I need his help. I also sensed somewhere deep down he feared he might have to take care of me. He never would because I am proud, and would never go that route, at least with someone who saw it as duty.

But winter was coming soon, and would I return to the city, or would I stay here and freeze or rent somewhere else?

I liked not knowing.

"I knew when I was in New York that you and Kurt would break up," he said. "He was not committed. You didn't live together. He didn't take care of you. I told you it was simply a relationship of two older people with no strings attached."

"Yes."

"What will you do now?" he asked.

He always asks me that in a most desperate way. What is going to happen to you, his voice frantic, and he always makes me feel as if I am about to fall off a cliff. It may well be, but I don't need it repeatedly drilled into my head. When you are falling off a cliff, you need optimism and creativity about how you might escape the fall, you don't need someone yelling, "You are falling off a cliff."

"I am not sure. I came here to figure it out," I said.

"Have you made any progress?"

"Not yet."

"I don't know how you can live like you do. You're like our father."

"Daddy always said something comes in at the last minute. I loved that," I said. "He was right, you know. And he kept working as long as he could. Which I intend to do."

"What about when you can't?"

"I'll deal with it then."

I was finding this discussion off-putting. It was so bleak. Like I was about to be shot or something.

"You know," I said, "during revolutions and wartime when people were going to be shot, they hugged even the people who were shooting them, to say goodbye to life."

He looked at me as if I were crazy.

"Want some lunch?" I asked.

We went to George's and George was voluble, asking my brother about life in Holland, and they got into the politics and my brother went on and on. Then he went on and on about the politics in the States, and then he finished off about the politics in the UK.

Lunch was long finished before this political forum ended.

I had hardly said a word and my brother did not ask my opinion.

I wished I had my glass heart to hold on to.

My phone rang. It was a man who had once published two books of mine. "That woman in Paris should bring your books out in France. They will sell better there."

"I agree. She intends to, I think."

"I will call her."

"Why don't you partner with her to bring them out if, you believe they will sell there?"

"Maybe I will," he said. "She should get a French partner."

"She says the French partners never make decisions. She'll like that you're American. My brother is here. Let's talk later."

I got off feeling a touch of hope. Something always comes in at the last minute, as my father said.

Chapter Forty-Two

My brother and I went on to discuss our parents a bit, one subject we did have in common, and went on to discuss what he does with his time now. He'd volunteered with the Olympics and lived in Korea for a while, while his wife stayed in Holland, and then he was on some long march with the US reserve military he was part of. He had pensions coming in from everywhere, which was intelligent, but, in our family way, he was on the move.

But his sadness for me made the day long, and soon he said he was taking the ferry back to get to London where he would meet a friend, and then back to Holland. Now I was sad because he was leaving, and I was glad at the same time.

We hugged, two vessels carrying the burden of our stories, but carrying on. He, in his mind, carrying on through his children and I, in my mind, through eternal inventions, if only for myself.

I watched the ferry go and we waved, and I realized I missed him. I felt such love for him.

I went back up the hill and listened to Count Basie in my mind. That tickle of the high notes as he slid around the piano. That ease and clarity. That taking his time to play the melody so it sounded simple but really so much was going on all over the piano, but the main melody so achingly perfect. Like a great conversation at times can be.

Then a knock.

Ah, good, I thought. It' s been a while. I grabbed my jacket and opened the door. "I could use a drink."

Skene stood tall and strong, trying to not give in to the laughter in his eyes.

"I hope it's more that you need than a drink," he said.

We went down to The Cavalier.

"I heard you had a friend visiting from the States," Skene volunteered.

"Yes," I said.

Then I thought he might know why Kurt left so abruptly. That he had gone off with one of Mrs. Shapiro's orphans. But then I thought who else would know that but me? On the other hand, that girl could have talked, and God knows who hears what. But then, that girl did not seem to mix in the same crowd as Skene.

"We parted badly," I said.

We had just reached The Cavalier. "Sorry to hear it."

"Are you?" I asked, my eyes teasing.

"Not particularly," he said, as we headed for his corner.

"Do you like Count Basie?" I asked.

"I do, but doesn't everyone."

The waitress brought over our drinks without asking. It was kind of warming.

It felt good to be with a friend. I looked at him, at his strong face, his steadiness. I decided he would be the one to teach me how to be touched.

"How is it going with your books?" he asked.

"I can't tell," I said. "My conflicting desire for them to come out coupled with my fear of them coming out cloud whatever is going on."

"I see," he said, therefore not telling me what he thought.

"My brother was just here."

"Ah, good visit?"

"Yes, I think. He likes to remind me doom is coming for me but, other than that . . . good. Maybe people want people who live free lives to pay, but we do, so what are they worried about?"

"What do you mean?"

"He thinks I am going to commit suicide due to poverty or, worse, end up on his doorstep."

Skene looked at me again with that way he had of looking at me as if I were a painting, which had the effect of making me feel pretty. Although, at my age, it seemed highly unlikely. "Well, if it comes to that, you can end up on my doorstep."

"What if you're married by then?" I asked.

"It's a large house."

I liked him for that. Kurt had never said that to me and I was his alleged girlfriend. He never said I could end up on his doorstep. It was what had driven me away. He would not rise to what really was going on inside me, which was a deep need to have a doorstep.

"There is a shrink word," I said to Skene, "called an anaclitic need. It is what drives you inside."

"I see. What is yours?"

"The shrink, whom I didn't particularly like or stay with, said that my anaclitic need was nurturance. I think this need means what you never got and thus are looking for. When you said that just now about your doorstep, it felt like you met my anaclitic need."

"A most peculiar way of saying thank you, but all right," he said.

"What's your anaclitic need?" I asked.

"Good question. To figure out how to trust someone. Is that a need?" He looked off.

"I would think so," I said.

My God, why hadn't I seen that Skene is reachable? "So, what is going on with you?" I asked.

"I bought a few more paintings. I went up to London for a bit."

"How is it you can afford such a life?"

"I came into a bit of money quite a long time ago."

"That's nice," I said.

"It was. Before that, I was, as you know, a doctor. But I think I mentioned that I like to take off a month or two each year to work in free medical practices in different countries."

"That is so wonderful."

"It certainly is for me," he said.

"Remind me, why did your wife leave you?" I asked, joking.

He laughed.

Some people came over and chatted about this piece of land being up for sale and how was his barn coming along and some discussion here and there about windows and wood, and did he know that Langton had died, and my heart bristled a bit about that, since I knew he'd died and something else had died along with it. "Yes, I did know," he said. "Sad story."

It was, I thought.

They left and he said, "And why did your American friend leave you? I don't see that much wrong with you either."

"He just wanted . . . more," I said.

"I can't imagine what that would be."

I didn't reply and looked out at the people. I didn't really want to know them. It is what had always kept me in a city, not having to see the same people over and over. Although I did see the same people over and over in the city.

As we walked home, we were silent, as was our habit. We listened to the water lapping from the harbor and the mournful sound of a lighthouse beacon scouring the sea.

We walked toward my place. I felt so comfortable next to him. Not excited, as I had been with Kurt, the excitement, it turned out, of wondering what and where things were, but here just comfortable since he was so even.

We got to my door and he said, "Well, good night then," and I turned to my place and then he grabbed my arm, strongly but gently, turned me back round toward him, and kissed me on the lips. I had forgotten what it is to be kissed on the lips. Kurt never did that, and it had been a long, long time. It shocked me but then I realized it felt so wonderful. I leaned toward him harder, and our kiss was longer perhaps than we both thought. I forgot that a kiss can flood your body with movement and desire.

I smiled at him. "That was," I said, "surprising."

He laughed.

"All right, then," he said, "sleep well." And he walked off.

That was surprising too.

I went into my dollhouse and looked for the glass heart. Where had I put it? I thought I might sleep with it, but I didn't have the energy to look for it under all my papers.

I'd find it in the morning. I climbed the ladder and couldn't remember in the morning how it was that I fell so gently asleep, as if in some kind of trance.

Chapter Forty-Three

I went to tennis and was matched up with some man, a younger man than Sir Leo, and he had this funny thing of doing a sideways slice where the ball looks like it's coming to you, but then abruptly goes sideways. Naturally a type like me misses.

Or he would just slam the ball so you couldn't hit it. I didn't quite understand the point of it because aren't we there to play? It just seemed to amuse him.

When we finished, there was a couple next to us in another court and my tennis partner looked at her and said, "Do you know who she is?"

"No."

"She's on television."

She was certainly physically strong. "Must be what it takes to be in the public eye," I said.

He snickered and went off.

I felt sad that I am an older woman. I thought all his tennis tricks were some kind of punishment for my not being young and pretty. Somebody in The Cavalier had taken a photo of Skene and myself and texted it to me. I held my phone up and was shocked to see my grandmother.

I would like to see my grandmother, of course, but not in me.

But then, I reminded myself as I walked back, that I had been kissed last night. Grandmothers don't get kissed like that, or do they?

* * *

I got home and there was a very tiny painting next to my door. A watercolor of a marsh with one tree on it and a large sky. I brought it in and put it on my windowsill. Thanks to Skene, my hovel became a home.

Chapter Forty-Four

Lucia came down the hill. It was getting near evening, and I was feeling a bit lonely, although sad that I was turning out to be so needy of attention. "Are you taking me out to dinner?" she asked out of the blue.

"Yes," I laughed. "Why not? Let's go."

She had her usual strange beak cap on and a scarf, and she looked pleased to be doing something different.

I held her arm to steady her as we walked to The Cavalier and was touched that she let me.

I remembered Skene holding mine on one of our first walks and how it had moved me so also.

People nodded to us, and she nodded to people as we went in, but she did not stop to talk. She is not a chatterer.

She ordered some wine, and I did too and, when the menu came, she suggested I order for her. I was not sure why, but I wondered if she could not see the type.

We both agreed on salads and then we both agreed England was not a place for salads and I said, "But I think they are better at them than they used to be."

She nodded. I told her about my brother having come.

"Do you have other brothers?" she asked.

"One in England. I was postponing seeing him till I felt fully strong."

She made no comment, as if what I said didn't make sense. Or maybe she did not want to talk about families and, in truth, neither did I. She then began talking about how she cannot tell me what she is writing about, but it is about what is going on in the world now. It would make things very clear.

I, as we know, was for some reason disturbed about what was going on in the world but did not know why I was. I just felt uneasy, but I noticed no one else did. I thought it was my overactive imagination and being suggestible to too much.

When I explained that to her, she replied, "It isn't that. You are feeling what is going on."

I knew that I couldn't ask her, "But what is going on?" She wasn't going to tell me.

I sat back.

"Just live as who you are," she said. "That is all you can do."

"I know."

And we both sipped our wines.

"How far is Topsham?" I asked George the next morning.

"Why?"

"I have another brother there and I thought I might go. Depending on how far it is."

"It's about two hours or so."

"Lovely."

"If he lives in Topsham," George said, "why have you waited this long to see him?"

I thought a minute. A good question, since I do adore this brother. I looked out the window and there was a man who had trouble with his legs walking by, with difficulty, as if he could fall any minute. George waved to him. I noticed the man was carrying a book. Made me so happy. That man can live a rich life.

I turned back to George. "I waited to see this brother for when I felt recovered enough from whatever was bothering me. I wanted to be in good shape. He matters to me."

"I see. How will you get there?"

"I haven't decided yet."

"Ask Skene to drive you."

"You do know, you're a bit of a matchmaker."

"And what if I am?"

And so it was that Skene and I were in his Jaguar, on the way to Topsham, a tiny fishing village. This brother distributes wines from there to the bars and restaurants in about a fifty-mile radius. This is a different brother, much younger, a so-called half-brother, but I always felt close to this one. I am the bigger sister, and he was at first my new doll, my willing audience when I wanted to watch him laugh. He is naturally kind and has a deep inner generosity and sweetness. When I used to visit him, he would drop me off at whatever airport I was leaving from, and he would stand and wait at the glass window overlooking the tarmac till the plane went off. I would see him all alone at the gate window. It touched me something immeasurable.

His good heart has a poetry to it, a humility of expansiveness.

It is always fun being in a car with a man. You have to engage together, or maybe it is a brief period of living together. Sometimes you are quiet, sometimes listening to music or the news, or other times talking. You discover how they drive. It tells you what they would be like to live with. Not surprisingly, Skene was a relaxed driver.

"I haven't been to Topsham in years," he said.

"Nor me," I said, looking out at the A4 motorway. It looked like any highway, in truth. My eyes roamed for those English hills with sheep on them and occasionally I would get a glimpse. "You'll like him and his wife. They are lively and easy to be with."

"Are you and your brother similar?"

"In some ways. Neither of us is competitive, I think, and probably we're both sensitive types. He has a warm heart. I am lucky to have him as a brother."

"I have one sister and we're friendly, but not enough to spend any time together," he said.

I thought that odd because clearly they came from money and you would think that would solve so many difficulties. Then I remembered money is probably one of the most common reasons for families falling apart.

We parked at a restaurant by the water that my brother and his wife had chosen. I was so happy to see Richard's tall handsome presence, his blondish hair and intelligent face, and he and Skene were similar in being thin and about the same height and they shook hands, almost like brothers themselves.

Karan said hello and gave me a look that she liked Skene's looks.

At lunch, she asked Skene about himself, and he said he did part-time doctoring, and collected art, and she said it sounded nice, but she sounded doubtful since part-time anything to her is sloth.

My brother joked that no matter how difficult times get, lockdowns, war, scarcity, wine is always good business.

I wanted to say, "A bit like doctoring," but that seemed obvious.

Karan said, "How long are you staying over here?"

"I am not sure."

Skene said, "She has these books that may come out in Paris."

"Oh?" my sister-in-law asked.

"Yes, a collection," I said. "It's a wild idea, and it is taking a lot out of me. Sometimes I don't know how the publisher is figuring this all out. But, of course, I know bigger presses than hers that are just as mysteriously nuts. So I just have to let go."

"Sort of exciting," my sister-in-law said with clipped lips. I know enough to know family hates when a member writes a book. For about a thousand reasons. What did she say about us? they wonder. What is she saying about anyone? And what if she gets famous, which I happened to know was highly unlikely with those books.

"Maybe exciting. Not sure," I replied. "How is your book coming?" Because, like many businesspeople, once they get some money, she had taken up writing. She will find out it is harder than being in business but let her enjoy her dreams, I thought, of the best-seller list. And what do I know? She has the success gene. She may get on the best-seller list.

"I am carrying on," she said, about her book.

In actuality, just the thought of my books, this collection, still made me pass out. My being so nakedly revealed to people reading them, if they did read them. I wished they would just be in French so no one I knew could read them.

This odd thing of writing and wanting the books to communicate and at the same time wanting to hide, which is why you write in the first place. "It is dizzying," I said, since I knew it would be a response to whatever question I might not have heard her ask.

At that moment, a French song came onto the PA system, "Ton Style" by Leo Ferre, a song about someone's style. Books are one's style. Another answer from out of nowhere.

I have to just detach detach detach from it, I told myself.

My brother suggested we four take a walk by the estuary and it was a good idea, and the sun was in and out of the clouds, the sun landing strange streaks of occasional gold on the water and on Skene and my brother ahead.

"Are you an item?" Karan asked me.

"Not really. Maybe. I don't know."

"You seem very compatible, or at ease with each other."

"Yes, well, it's because he's very nice. But he reveals himself slowly, which makes me do the same. Or maybe I am revealing the real me and that is a slow process. Who knows?"

"How's Kurt?"

"I don't know."

"Well, I suppose nobody does know him," she replied.

I laughed.

"I used to enjoy our dinners," she said, "with him, but I could never really figure out what he was saying."

"Maybe he couldn't either," I said.

"Why have you left New York and come here?" she asked. "I can't imagine you living this life."

"To do something completely different. I had to."

"Well, you're getting on. At some point you have to be sensible." When she said things like this, I always thought she was Margaret Thatcher.

"It's a bit late to start being sensible, isn't it?"

She smiled ruefully. Another one perhaps frightened I will end up at her door.

"Well, are you finding anything out," she asked, "with this new adventure?"

"How to play Chopin," I said. "I'm learning it with a 100-year-old possible conductor, and I think I am going to let Skene teach me how to stay still when I am being touched."

"Very practical, as usual," she replied.

We laughed.

Skene and my brother had magically turned up at our sides. My brother had heard the last exchange, and, God bless him, he sidled up to me, put his hand on my arm, and smiled at me as if to say, "I'm here."

Chapter Forty-Five

Skene and I stopped off for dinner at a pub he knew on the way back that was an old farmhouse situated in a fulsome English garden, with little bridges across brooks, and then inside calm and pretty and tender and the waiters had humor and I sat back and relaxed in a way I hadn't in so long.

My phone rang.

"Maybe we left something with them," I said to him, looking for my phone, but, when I looked at it, it was Irene in Paris. "I probably should take this. My apologies."

I stood up and went outside with the phone into what now looked like almost a watercolor garden of pastel greens.

"Things are moving, dear," she said. "I think we can begin."

Normally this would be good news.

"Wonderful," I said, but she was too smart to not hear the truth.

"Don't worry, everything will go well."

"We should send stuff out for reviews. In far Samoa or somewhere," I joked.

"We'll send them out to proper places."

"Well, then . . ."

"And I am looking for ways to get the books out in French."

I just stood there. "Well, thank you. Thank you for all of it," I said. Why does she sound so happy? We may be about to commit suicide.

"Something's happening," she said. "Your work, dear. Your work. You've done the work."

"Yes. Thanks again. Let me know how I can help."

I sat back down with Skene. "Good news?" he asked.

"I don't know. My fate has left my hands."

"Should I order champagne?"

"No."

We were quiet, then I added, "All my mistakes and flaws are now flaunted in front of anyone who has the bad luck to read one of these books."

"Well, Anna Karenina made some mistakes."

"I don't think they were Tolstoy's. Maybe they were ones he wanted to make. Mine are mine. How could I be so stupid?"

"It's probably not as bad as you think."

"Well," I said, "one of my characters goes to prison to atone for his sins. I guess I might be going public to atone for mine."

"What is it exactly you are guilty of?" he asked cheerily, as if I could not possibly be guilty of crimes.

"I was so mixed up I was cruel to those who loved me."

"Everybody is guilty of that."

"That is what I thought when I wrote the books." I smiled glumly. "But I am not sure everyone was so cruel repeatedly, and with such gusto."

I looked out the window at the pastoral fields, when we were back in the car, the ancient trees dotting the landscape, and I thought quietly once again about why I was so far away from everything.

I had read the news in the morning. Bezos banning "hate" books and documentaries that do not ally to his politics. More executive orders being signed in forty-one days than three presidents before him put together and nobody knows what's in them.

I have to be open to change, I told myself. I have to be open that the country I emigrated to is becoming another country.

"Why are you so upset?" Kurt had said when I once brought it up when I was still in New York. "Things always change.

England, Rome—all of them lost their power," Kurt had said when I was trying to understand the news.

And he's a Republican.

"I don't know," I said.

"It's because you had an unstable childhood. You believed in the institutions here."

It was a strange analysis, hard for me to believe I believed in any institution, I hadn't even been willing to go to college, seeing no value, perhaps incorrectly, in institutions, but I couldn't totally dismiss what he said.

I turned to Skene, who was looking around companionably, waiting for me to return to our conversation. I said, "Your island is unchanging, or to me it is. It is just beauty and people, and I don't feel anyone is obsessing about how awful someone else is, or maybe they are, and I have absolutely no touch with it, and I think that is what I needed. People don't seem to be maneuvering, I mean."

"Well, when you live here it's all the same human dramas, you know. Envy, infidelity, an argument over where the fence goes, picking up after your dog. I think what you're saying is there is time or room for happiness and perhaps that is not true in every life. But it's not paradise, and I do find it rather amusing how you are seeing it like that. It sort of makes me see it like that, and that is almost enriching to me!"

I smiled.

Then he said, "I thought everyone hated Trump, and all is renewed over there now."

"They do. But it may be six of one, half a dozen of the other. I had no idea how much power means to everyone. Machievelli was right. People will do or say anything to get it."

He said nothing.

"Maybe I just hold on to things," I said. "The past."

"A writer's terrain," he said.

"If you're Proust, which I'm not."

He put his hand on mine. "Don't worry so. You'll mend here. Till you're ready to go out again."

I wondered if he could mend my heart; after all, he is a doctor. While he was at it, could he mend my fear of being touched? I looked down at his hand on mine and let him keep it there.

"Why don't you sleep at my place to night?" he said. "For one thing, it will be warmer, and one can walk across a room. For another, it has a real bed."

"And there is you." I smiled.

"The piece de resistance."

We drove in silence, me thinking. Am I ready to start something? It would change our friendship, into what? I looked out the window and knew I was indeed frightened of starting something new. I, who am always longing for the new.

He looked at me thinking and then looked away.

"Yes, terrible things could happen," he said.

I smiled.

More silence.

"I can't quite do it yet," I said.

"All right," he said. "There's no hurry."

"I feel like such a coward."

"It's not like fighting for the republic," he said. "It just happens when you feel like it. When we're young, we always feel like it."

True, I thought.

"Actually," I said, "I know a man in New York who, for some reason, hires hookers. I wonder what they do."

In truth, I found it unattractive of that man, but I know most men do it or want to.

The simplicity of it.

I grimaced.

I had written a book for a hooker. It was a profession to her, and there were endless clients. She prided herself on her good service. She had good reviews. It turns out there is a place that has Yelp-like reviews for hookers. She is very pretty and not young. Forty but looks young. She is always getting new breasts. She is very thin. A sort of young Catherine Deneuve. She claims to really like sex. Did I ever? I can't remember.

I hadn't for so long.

And yet I like sleeping with a man. I like a man's body and I like being near it. Why didn't I like sex, I wondered. I think I did when young.

"What if I just slept over," I said, "and we see what happens."

"Well, that was the general idea," he replied.

"Yes."

So we drove to his house. I went in, George the dog greeted us, we had a drink, and I looked at the new painting he had bought with me in Paris. He had not hung it but put it on top of a table, leaning against a wall, and it looked good there. A ray of life lighting the room. The blue, white, and orange did that. I studied it. He came up behind me and put his arms around me. It felt so peaceful.

"Let's go upstairs," he said. "It's late."

"All right."

"I actually have to leave early in the morning," he said, "to get to a clinic in Cheltenham."

"Okay," I said, meaning, Good, I will be alone to process all this.

We went upstairs to an open but warm bedroom that looked out over the sea. "There's a spare toothbrush in the bathroom," he said, pointing.

"How come?" I asked.

"I don't know."

I took in the neatness of the bathroom, the overall comfort

of everything, like I fit in, rugged but elegant, and brushed my teeth, checked to see if he had any moisturizer. Kurt always did but Kurt was a metrosexual. Colognes, moisturizers, eye creams, shampoos, toners. He couldn't stop himself from ordering things for himself.

I came back into the bedroom.

I could see which side he slept on because of the books and pens and paper. At least no sleep apnea paraphernalia, I thought. No apothecary of pills, as I had once seen in a man's apartment. So odd learning a man's world. It is how you decide.

What would a man decide about me in Lucia's house or anywhere I lived? They'd think me bookish, unconventional, a lousy homemaker.

I went to the other side of the bed. I can't say I felt lustful. Had I ever, I once again wondered.

I took off my clothes. Kurt had liked me dressed, au habille, had never paid much attention to my body. When young, I had a nice body, good breasts, but now they had fallen, not grotesquely, but they were no longer something to be proud of, and I still had a waist, actually my body wasn't bad for an older woman but I did have those wrinkles in my arms, tennis made my legs not bad, but I don't know, I didn't know what to think, what am I doing here—

Skene said, "You're quite beautiful. I've always liked slender women."

I got under the covers and what I did feel was when he got in, I wanted to be close to him. That came out of nowhere. I just clung to him, with no space anywhere. My body wanted to.

It wasn't desire for sex, it was desire for him.

At this point, that was all I wanted, and God bless him, he understood.

Chapter Forty-Six

In the morning, he made toast, tea, and fruit.

"Do you want a shower?" he asked.

"I can do so at Lucia's."

He made no comment, but maybe he understood that taming me would have to be in stages.

"I'll have to buy coffee if you're going to be coming here," he said.

"I can pick it up," I replied. "Or I can always swing by George's."

Speaking of George's, George the dog now liked to play with me and spent his time coming over for petting and attention, which I enjoyed giving. I love dogs so much more easily than their owners.

We sat in silence but smiled and already I felt I belonged with him, the owner. Then he said, "I better go. I'll see you later."

"Okay," I said, and soon I was on my way to the other George's to pick up a coffee. He wasn't there, which was good, I didn't quite want to be questioned, and the person tending the restaurant wasn't the least bit interested in me and I took the coffee up to Lucia's tiny house. It was not lost upon me that George had ordered "takeaway" cups for me.

I got back, took a shower, and then sat at my table and opened the email. The woman in Paris wanted to know how preparing for the new podcasts were going, and I looked at the microphone she'd sent, which takes up practically the whole place. Thank God Amazon goes everywhere, even here, so I was able to get a stand, the mic, earphones, all of it.

"All good," I said, and then sat back and looked out to the sea. I didn't feel so on edge, as I usually did. Partially it was Skene and taking a minor risk as I had, and also it was that I was beginning to come to terms. I come from, for better or worse, a white ethos, and here I had come to the place of so much "evil," meaning Great Britain, where the sun never set at one time.

I knew, even when I was small, that being born white was lucky. Or seemingly, in a white world, uncomplicated. I also knew it was colder. And I was now watching that world going, going, gone. And, actually, all these people mixing up together is a great thing. Other cultures are more family oriented, less acquisitive, at least so far, and more relaxed than white people.

I will miss all that, the new type of people being born, when I bump off. Mine was a life of separation. A loss of richness for my generation.

Now, it did not seem so much as I was off key, it just seemed I should step aside gracefully in some way, being old and white.

I should go with it. As I should maybe go with Skene.

I trudged off to Sir Leo's, who probably does not worry much about change. He has only two big changes to worry about. Illness and the ensuing outcome, and I suspect he only worries about the first.

It was odd taking piano lessons when I did not practice. Sir Leo had mentioned moving a piano into Lucia's tiny house, but I was not sure I would be staying long enough to warrant such a futile exercise. I had thought that I could ask someone who did have a piano to let me practice there, but then I would be in another relationship and that was not why I came here.

I began the long walk to Sir Leo's, as always beautiful, and it happened it was warmer today, which made my journey optimistic.

My phone rang and it was the film director I liked working with.

"I signed the distribution agreement," he said, "but I have some interesting news for you."

"Yes?" I said, the sea lilting quietly beside me.

"They are translating the film into French, and it will be in France, and I told your publisher and she is pushing one of your books into French so the film and the book can help each other."

"Great." Really? I thought. Could that really happen?

He said as a sort of amend to me, "Your idea of three stories in one film was a good idea. It is livelier."

"Yes," I said.

But who knows. I am just as often wrong about what works. Irene in France and our early podcasts had worked even though I was suspicious of the whole idea. Who would want to listen? I thought they would turn out dull, but people allegedly were getting something out of them.

That was why it was good Irene was leading the way. I had to get out of the way gracefully there too.

I was at Sir Leo's. The door opened as it usually does.

He had Benjamin Britten in his hands. "Let's go," he said.

"Those are string quartets," I replied.

"I will play the violin, you play the piano. This is transcribed that way."

"I am not good enough to accompany you."

"You, my dear girl, have no idea of what you are good or not good at. I have learned that much about you. The trick is not to listen to anything you say, and I would advise you not to listen to anything you think."

A relieving thought. "Good idea."

* * *

He immediately had us sit down at the piano. I had found Sir Leo's furor. As we set up, I thought I could love this man. Who does not love a man of furor? I realized I was falling in love with all the men here.

"All right," he said, "don't worry about me. I am versed enough to play along with you no matter what mistakes you make. Too fast, too slow, wrong notes. So just do your best."

"Okay."

I began to play. I happen to love Benjamin Britten.

The piano part was quite simple, almost what a child would play. He was the one who had all the heavy bowing. High notes, plucking at notes, going from high to low like a zither, then back up, then plucking, back and forth, more plucking, a veritable orchestra in his capable hands.

It was almost like a performance I was attending, with me adding in a few complementary notes.

He finished with a powerful bowing, and I thought I was off the hook for a lesson but then he pulled out some Messiaen Etudes. I grimaced inside although I was a little curious. I liked Messiaen's Quartet for the End of Time. As usual we did only about seven notes with two hands, because Sir Leo admires perfection, and it takes a lot for me to even get near perfection and it didn't matter because the piece is quite beautiful. *Les Sons Impalpables du Rêve*. Appropriate, I thought. There was a kind of insistent structure to the music and occasional light trills that were like an eternal return. It was good for the soul, and then it was time for our silver tray and silver decanter by the open window overlooking the afternoon sun on his trees and garden.

"You seem a bit cheerier today," he said.

"I've figured some stuff out."

"Oh? Anything you can report on?" he asked, taking a sip of his gloaming hour cocktail.

"Well, I came to this island, obviously, because I was out of sorts. Perhaps most likely with my personal life. But I also felt that I had to in some way process for myself what was going on around me. I used to take the news and the arts and their obsession with change and new language and repression of the old as an affront. But I now realize it had nothing to do with me, it's just the world moving to the preoccupations of a larger, growing diverse world. I am now able to accept it is not some kind of act of political aggression, which is how the news divulges it." I even threw in a non sequitur. "That sexual fluidity, as an example, is nothing new, Greece, perhaps the Neanderthals, who knows."

He didn't reply.

I continued, "This place will change, too."

"True. Everything does, especially ourselves."

"I was fighting it."

"Your way, I suppose."

We sat in silence, just enjoying the breeze and the quiet.

"This won't change, I hope," I said, moving my hand toward the window.

"Climate people think it will," he said.

"Yes. Everything is changing out there, even the Earth, allegedly, and I am trying to integrate that into my psyche."

"But, my dear girl, change has always been going on."

"Yes, I know. But slower. And not so in your face. And not so loud with all the news vehicles—"

"Believe me, it was loud. The fascists and Blackshirts were loud—"

"True."

"The Blitz was loud. The poverty was loud. The takeover of countries was loud."

"True."

"This evolution," he said, "is life. Sometimes unpleasant, sometimes pleasant, but one gets through with what matters to you. One fights for what one believes in but in the end what matters are your own integrity and what you love, what you see as adding to the good of the world. In my case, music. Books, in your case. Natural beauty for most people. Political change for some. Medical research for others. Science. Whatever is our bailiwick. We hold on to those. There's plenty of beauty in that, and look how long I've lived because of the fact I have been doing what I was meant to. I had my difficulties, of course, many of the same things you speak of, changes in language or how a government is run, or just the terrible thing of seeing how awful people can be, it never stops shocking and it does, it does terrible damage to the psyche, both of the person being done to and the person watching or doing it, but art, dear, and love and nature and integrity, my God, integrity counterbalance it. Forgive me for being banal."

"It's not banal," I said. "I know it sounds so, but it is indeed all we have to hold on to."

"Lucia has God," he said, "but that is her art."

I nodded. Odd, I thought, that he brings up Lucia.

"Do you know her well?"

"Yes," he said, "everyone knows everyone here in some way or another."

Chapter Forty-Seven

I came back and lay down on the mattress in the loft. Took my laptop and put on a station with Irish music. That percussive dance beat and the sound of female voices like angels haunting, urging us on, go forth, go forth.

Their pulsing chanting inspired me to jump up and race out to the bridge to cross over to the other side of the harbor, the female Gaelic voices in my ear. Skene had stood beside me that first day as I looked over the harbor. I would go exactly there. It was part of the reason I had come here.

I ate a fig bar as I trudged across, a fig bar Lucia had left me. Figs. Jerusalem.

Gaelic voices reminded me of my ex-husband, whom I knew I would eternally love. He adored their harmonies. "Let's play that record, Enya." What happened to Enya, I wondered.

I was also walking to not be there at my laptop receiving those constant emails, asking for money for one political party or the other. All written as if the sky is falling, and what the other party is doing is the end of the earth, each party accusing the other of being evil, and as I looked around at the hills, the trees, the sea, I saw it wasn't the end. Why are they raising money by telling us everything is over? I was so tired of this invasion of hateful alarmism.

Maybe they were changing the world for the better, who knows? What is wrong with a kinder world, I asked myself, one where everyone should be able to fit in. But why is the path to get there so nasty? Yet Sir Leo had told me that he'd read that young people nowadays help each other on social networking. He found it very moving. They pay each other's rent, even people who don't know each other. It is the beginning of socialism, and the better part.

Hadn't I spent most of my life worrying about money and doing bizarre things, like selling fish boxes to fish piers, dressing up as a Breton maiden to waitress, being nice to bosses who were just leering idiots, to pay my rent? No wonder these people want something where you don't have to demean yourself to make money. A gentler world than capitalism. But then socialism in Cuba and Russia were and are not kinder, and that was why my mind kept wrestling.

I had reached the other side of the harbor. The Gaelic voices louder in my ear. Sail Away! Sail Away! Sail Away!

As I continued walking the publisher texted me about a woman starting a woman's voices network. Getting louder, I thought.

A racket, and am I contributing?

I got to the harbor edge and looked across at the town, if you could call it that. Still inviting and glowing in the sun. I stood there, looking across, and felt moved that I had been drawn here, not even knowing that it housed George with his cheery advice and coffee, Lucia listening to God, Skene with his steadiness, and Sir Leo with his music and immortality. They were a mighty army, I thought. I must not give up, I told myself, no matter how many people think I am doomed.

I did sail away! Sail away!

Every day there is a new reason I am here and every reason as it becomes known to me and thought out is like taking off one more article of weight.

I looked down at the water and it had been to my right that I had seen the dead fishermen. I was avoiding looking in that direction, but I braced myself for the shocking image. I told myself to buck up and look down, and so I prepared myself, for there is something so personal about looking at dead people, the ultimate confrontation. I reminded myself that philosophers and artists often kept skulls on their desks as a call to live, live now, and I drew my breath deeply, turned, looked down, and they were not there.

Thank God. What did they're not being there mean?

Why, why do we forget we are dying? It is nice of course that we do forget, and yet when people find out they are dying, life seems more precious. I had to remember that. A friend writes in her book about dying with no regrets. My mind skitters away from the sentence. I suppose because I always thought this an impossibility. To live is to hurt people, if only inadvertently. How can we not regret that? Not to mention regret the many roads not taken, for all of us. The conventional road does ensure one of much, if you happen to be conventional. A family. A home. Assets to be left to next generations. Those who take the conventional road do live full lives, betting on family as the fullness, and the supporting of that family as equity. An unconventional road, such as mine, encompasses skittering and a bit of going back and forth. I'll try this road, no, this one.

I had met a woman who taught internationally. She spoke eight languages and moved from continent to continent. She had a capacity, one supposes, to be alone. It sounded amazing, what she did. I complimented her.

"Why don't you do it?" she asked.

I began walking back to the house. The fishermen were gone, having made their point, time's fishing for our souls, our limited time in the sea of our life, gone to lodge inside me.

Chapter Forty-Eight

I was on hold with Match.com in Lucia's dollhouse to sign up the widow down the street. She doesn't have a computer but wants to meet someone, so I am doing it for her. I will answer her suitors on the computer, if she gets any, and tell them to phone her.

But for some reason Match is blocking this idea. So here I am on the phone to them to find out why, listening to piped-in music on the phone that would make Sir Leo's skin crawl.

They are going to call me back.

Skene came that evening and said, "Let's go for a walk." It was a warm night, gentle, the cold not coming on yet, and we strolled easily by the sea. The few lights in the area rippling over the water. The stationary boats riding the tide, waiting to go to work the next day.

"How was your day?" he said.

"Lovely. I saw Sir Leo, but I need to get more work."

"I thought you were writing that play for that woman who has a hard life."

"I am, but I meant moneymaking work."

"You could help Sir Leo."

"No, I couldn't. I am as messy as he is."

"Well, no one could not have a mess in Lucia's house. It's so small."

"Some people would keep it very tidy," I argued.

Why are we talking about this?

"What about you? Did you save any lives today?"

"I hope so. But the cases are hardly that dramatic. I am not in an emergency room, you know. More it's about the grippe and having a hangover."

I laughed and took his arm. "Where are we walking to, by the way?"

"Not sure yet. Let's just walk. It's so lovely by the harbor," he said. And it was, and as I looked out at the trusty boats bobbing away, I imagined them going off to pick up the soldiers at Dunkirk. Little soldiers themselves. The thought of it always made me cry.

"What will you do about work?" he asked.

"I may have to take a quick trip to the States to try and make some money on someone else's book. Or maybe something will come in here."

At this point he was holding my hand.

"Well, if you go, I hope you don't end up staying there."

I smiled politely but bristled inside. Then I took my hand back.

As I said, you take yourself with you when you go.

Chapter Forty-Nine

This woman for whom I am writing a play has a habit, a bit like Lucia, of discussing all her problems with God. She gets answers that way. God seems to lead her to what she needs to do next. She prays for things, and she gets them. She also gets a lot of bad luck, three children in prison, but God told her how to earn enough for the lawyers and the innocent son was released. In her case, God seems to know what He is doing.

She and Lucia had tough early lives. God the entity they can trust.

I think what this woman I am writing for does is not give up hope. And she does not listen when people say something is not possible. She throws her hat into the ring and keeps throwing. She is not deterred by what people say. Only listens to God. And something happens.

I could stand to pay attention.

Skene popped over once during the day dropping off lunch as I constructed the play. I thanked him and wondered out loud if it was possible for me to write in the woman's Philadelphia vernacular. Could I get the music of it?

"She'll add that in as she performs it," he said.

Yes, I thought, and off he went, and off I went to the play.

The next day he asked if I wanted to relax with a movie at his place with him and his dog, the other George. Maybe a movie about the same subject I am writing about, he suggested.

"No," I said. "I don't want to be influenced."

He said nothing, having been someone who had been schooled to be influenced.

I found myself getting used to his visits.

And he seemed to also like what was becoming a routine. I liked how he hung about a bit talking about the windows on the barn, the landscaping, he might start looking at sculpture, asking about what I was doing without telling me what to do, which was what Kurt always did. I liked his uniform of a woolen sweater and cap, and how he was happy to go off himself, busy, it seemed, if only fixing something for that widow down the street.

I saw now he had a kinetic energy of his own, and it was starting to hook into mine.

Chapter Fifty

Time for my piano lesson and, just as wonderfully, the walk there. Gulls were busily instructing me on the rest of my life, the sun was in and out, the sea was steady, and the trees were showing off. Where was the famous English rain? Obviously, in Spain. A veritable party as I made my way there.

Then the cypresses, as habit, welcomed me and whispered, "On to the open door, madame."

"What is it today?" I asked gaily as I walked in.

"No piano," he said.

"What do you mean?"

"I had to have some kind of shot and I am a bit dizzy, nothing serious, but no piano."

"Oh, maybe I shouldn't be bothering you and you can rest."

"Plenty of rest coming up for me later," he replied.

I looked at him.

"You don't know that expression?" he asked. "It's Japanese. Take rest after death."

"Yes, I am in accord with that."

"Undoubtedly."

"You're English," I said. "Why don't you have a dog?"

"Who said I was English?"

"True. Lucia does not think you are."

"Lucia . . ."

"Do you know her well?" I tried again. Something told me he did.

He looked out the window. "Yes, but I think I am dead to her."

I was shocked. "Why?"

"I knew her when she was a young woman. Very beautiful and a marvelous spirit, although she doesn't have a clue about music. The kind of person who waves her hand along as she listens. Horrible. But she did and probably still does have a kind of perfectionism about her"—I looked up at him, an interesting word, I thought, but he kept on talking—"an energy, and she has a strange high-born quality about her even though she lost her parents and had to be raised by a dressmaker. It was inherent."

"She is quite spiritual," I said.

"Yes, she always liked to be in high society, and I always used to tell her that she must think this talking with God she does all the time is hobnobbing with the highest society she can get in with. She would laugh."

"You seem to love her," I ventured.

Again, he looked off. "Yes, that might be true."

"Well, why don't you go out with her? You're both available. And you're what they call in the States geographically compatible, or something like that."

"Well, if you must know, Lucia was my wife before my last wife."

I was a bit shocked and quiet for a minute. Then I said, "That shouldn't make any difference."

"It's true. One never stops loving someone you once loved, but it is hard to go back."

"Did you come here because of her?" I asked, now sitting down.

"That's what's funny," he said, sitting down across from me, too. "I didn't. But it shows that one you love often has the same taste or sense of value as yourself. Is moved by the same things, so I am not particularly surprised we found ourselves here in this almost glorious place together."

I didn't know what to say.

Then I came out with, "I think you should try to see her."

"Why?" he asked. "I have plenty to do. Sometimes loving from a distance is absolutely enough, especially as you get older."

"I don't know if that's so or not, but"—I looked away—"I probably am not one to be giving love advice."

"Probably not," he said, looking out the window. "But then again, no one is."

"Probably not." I too looked out the window, then back at him. "I find it odd Lucia does not check up on you and have you as a friend."

"Lucia is a person who doesn't need many people. One can only hope she prays for me."

"Yes." I smiled. "I am sure she does."

"And what about you, young lady?"

"I hope she prays for me too."

He laughed and said, "Well, you're right, I should lie down. I apologize you came all the way over here. I have never asked you for your phone number."

"I enjoy the walk, as you know, so it was most enjoyable, and I did get the pleasure of a glimpse of you and get to hear your most unusual revelation."

"Well, we can talk about that another time."

I stood up and kissed his cheek and said, "As the old American Westerns like to say, I'll be back."

"Good," he said, and shut the door.

Chapter Fifty-One

On the walk home I decided to cross the bridge again to the other side of the harbor, just to check once more about the fishermen. I wanted to understand how this vision I had seemed to also have appeared to other people.

As I walked, I thought about Sir Leo and Lucia. It did seem like a love of some kind had put them on the same island. Some inner thread. Why aren't they friends? Maybe Lucia with her love of God likes the thread of existing in the ether, not that concerned with matters here on Earth. And Sir Leo doesn't seem particularly lonely, nor does she. Their own lives are filled up enough, it seemed. He with his garden, classical books, and piano. Lucia with transcribing her books on biblical symbols.

I got to the edge of the sea where I had first seen the town. I noticed a figure moving on the bridge and I squinted to see who, and who should be walking across the bridge right now toward me but Skene? Walking quickly, it seemed. I did not look down at the fishermen in case I saw them again, it was such a terrifying thought, so I turned and walked toward Skene, his long corduroy-covered legs striding vigorously, wearing his sweater and cap as usual, the effect being a young man.

"What are you doing here?" I asked.

"I thought I'd accompany you on your walk."

"How did you know I was here?"

He turned and pointed to his house on the hill.

"Oh."

"It's a lovely view from here," he said. "I come here myself. I thought it curious you were on this side."

"This is where I met you," I ventured. "Don't you remember?"

"No," he said. "You met me that day I helped you with your bag at the dock."

I rubbed my neck. "I thought you said we did meet here."

He looked at me oddly.

Am I losing my mind?

We began walking toward the hill, without words, to the place where I felt I had first seen the town, the fishermen, even him.

"It's funny, I am sure I met you there," I said, pointing to the lookout.

"Impossible."

"Why? You said you like this view. You may have forgotten you met me here."

"I don't think I would forget. What did we talk about?"

"Nothing," I said. "I don't think we spoke. Maybe you didn't notice me."

"Unlikely. You're too vivid."

That annoyed me. They used to say pretty. Well, so much for that.

"Are you distracted by something?" he asked.

"Yes, I thought I saw dead fishermen in the water that day we met here that you are saying never happened. I also thought you had mentioned them, even a few times."

"In the case of seeing dead fishermen in the water, that is highly highly highly unlikely."

I turned to him. "Are you saying I am going mad?"

"I am not. But there is a thing," he said.

"What thing?"

"Well, when you live in a place like this, your inside thoughts become your outside thoughts. There is no difference between the inner and the outer. What is in your thoughts seems fully alive and visible."

"In a magical realism way?"

"No, just that there is the space for that to happen. What one hears internally can present itself as real. It is why people stay. I think that is the real reason you came. You wanted that."

I stared out at the view.

"Wanted what?"

"Your inner life to run your outer life."

"Oh, Skene," I said, and took his arm. Maybe he is mad too, I thought.

"You know, there's a lovely Italian restaurant around here, one I can conjure up," he said, eyes smiling, "where not everyone knows me, thank God. Why don't we go and have dinner? It's getting toward evening."

"Excellent," I said. "I hope the drink is not imaginary."

We began walking to another little town with one high street, and I saw they had a nails place. I hadn't had a manicure since I got here. It is how one relaxes in New York.

"Have you got a book on you?" I asked.

"No."

"Well, I want to get a manicure, I need one, and—"

"It's all right. Go ahead. I can read the newspaper. Meet me at da Umberto."

While getting my manicure, I checked my emails on my phone and saw that the widow down the street had a few gentlemen callers now that I had put her on a dating site. I had to answer the winks and flirts. There was a bit of action around her, no one close by, but one offered to move if it worked out and another was willing to drive from London.

The young Welsh woman finished my nails and they looked pretty and clean, and then I got directions to da Umberto.

Skene had found a little table in the corner and stood up and pulled the chair for me when I sat down. I felt like a princess. Not something American men do.

The restaurant was playing Bach piano music. I wondered if Sir Leo had been here.

Maybe I should invite him.

"When do you go to New York?" Skene asked.

"On Tuesday."

He looked off. "I wonder if you will actually come back."

For some reason, I experienced that as plaintive and possessive and once again I felt myself bristle. I need to work, I told myself. It isn't more complicated than that. There is no hope for me with someone who doesn't understand that.

"You know I have to go back to work," I said.

All of a sudden, Kurt with his eternal distance looked very attractive.

"I had wanted to take you to the Cotswolds," he said.

"Well," I replied impatiently, "we can do that another time."

He noticed my impatience.

"Why are you biting your new nails," he asked.

It was good that he pointed it out; it distracted me from making a snide remark. I took my hand out of my mouth, but, nonetheless, something in us was clashing.

To get onto neutral ground, I asked him about his paintings, the barn, people in the area, and listened, but I didn't want to be there, and he knew it. I felt profoundly trapped and annoyed.

This is what happened when a man wanted me. I would do anything to get away. Eternal recurrence.

"You might be annoyed that you have to go," he said, as if he could hear my thoughts. "That you have to worry about work all the time."

I hesitated before I said anything because it was possible that was why I was angry but a part of me also wanted to go. I had a life in New York that I couldn't just dispense with as if it had never existed. Now it seemed somewhat attractive for some reason.

Rather like a dog who lies down when he or she does not want to fight, I said, "I don't know."

Chapter Fifty-Two

First, I took a train to get the plane from London to Miami, where I was to see a client who needed some revisions on what I had written for her years back. It felt so good to be in motion with my laptop. The two of us together on the road. We were so steadfast a team.

The seats on the train were comfortable and I'd had a coffee beforehand to make the trip festive.

I had editing to do, and I did it.

Then at the airport check-in, the whole nonsense, then the futile shopping and eating snacks I would never normally eat such as potato chips and chocolate, and then settling into the plane and the comfort of being alone and inaccessible.

It felt like home.

When I was on wireless on the plane, I found some more men for the widow down the street. When I got to Miami, I called her with the phone numbers for her to call them.

I prayed she would meet someone good, but I say that as an expression.

This woman I was meeting in Miami regarding her book was, like Lucia, completely absorbed in God.

I had tried to talk about it with Skene.

"Is it because they had no one as children and one has to have hope, so God is available for that?"

He nodded.

"So, when they attribute things that to them are miraculous and maybe they are but all of life is a bit of a miracle really, are they actually simply just trying to interpret the miraculous?"

He looked at me with his dark eyes and his voice was intense. "You know, my former wife said she once heard a voice telling her to be a schoolteacher and she turned around and began the schooling to become one. And I think she would say she is happy she did that. She said she was told by a voice."

"Yes, that's what they all say."

He made no comment; after all, what more was there to say on the subject? I could mention that I think it was Fanon, not the revolutionary but the French philosopher, who said the proof of God was the desire for God.

I could have said that to Skene, but I didn't. Maybe it has been said enough.

Chapter Fifty-Three

Now I was back in America, passing large screens in the airport with Tucker Carlson saying Biden was doing terrible things behind the scenes, and, not wanting to get sucked in, I checked my emails as I walked, only to see a note from publishers asking if I knew any writers of color. Cuomo was a star when I left, and now, I saw on another screen in the airport, he was being spoken of as a pariah. I was back in America, where it is sport to denigrate the other.

That interminable happy music piped in. A conspiracy not to think. As I walked, I saw so much food, so much makeup, wine, clothing, everything for sale. And if you passed a kiosk, here is another one thirty feet ahead with almost the same offerings. Maybe this time you will buy. As Lenin had it, repetition is everything. Maybe all these people go inward to God or to a small town as I did to get away from this constant pull to exteriorization. It is around us all the time, shiny things as if we are mice.

My client here is Cuban, and I was not sure if she would be considered a person of color but I decided to recommend her book to the publisher and see if that qualified. I wrote Paris to find out.

I already missed the walks from where I came. I may have been given a glass heart there but here people were walking so quickly, I couldn't feel any hearts. But look, already I am American and judging, just as they are.

I searched my handbag for a book that I had not read as planned, since I'd had to edit on the plane to pay for my many wolves at the door. The book is by Natalia Ginzberg and not the most interesting book I have ever read but it is pure of heart, so I was keeping it close. Interestingly, the book I was editing on the plane was also not particularly interesting. Ginzberg was much more sophisticated, witty and a beautiful writer, and the book I was editing had none of those traits, but it was very honest, a cry to be heard as the writer exposed all his sores and demons, and somehow that cry kept one reading.

I got an Uber once I'd walked through the airport. The car was big and lush. A Punjab driver, a Sikh, and I wanted to tell him how I respect his faith so much but I didn't want to sound like a valley girl. He was elegant in his bearing, and I knew so many of their rituals, how in India on the full moon they go to these places where all Sikhs eat together, no matter what caste, and are by the water and are community, praying or not praying together. I said to him since his car was so clean and elegant, "I wish you could drive me somewhere far away." He didn't comment. We drove through neighborhoods on my way to the client and I saw, because of the nice weather, people were standing round in their driveways, just talking, and, all of a sudden, I was seeing bigger "things." Bigger cars and all the paraphernalia that goes with them. Three cars in a driveway. Still, there was that wonderful American optimism. You too can have anything you want if luck favors you or you find where luck is.

And the sun, the sun heating up my own car and everything was hot out there, too. It made me aware it had been a soft quiet intermittent sun I had been living under the past few months. Here it was blazing. This client too is a God client, and she once said the Miami blue sky is the color of the Virgin.

The Uber driver was playing *The Phantom of the Opera* on

his radio. That ethereal music. The characters' obsession with music. I suddenly felt that I too must be a person with a mask since I had myself turned away from the garish light of day in Lucia's hut and listened to the music of the night when on the island.

It did not end well for the Phantom, I reminded myself. Or maybe he just ends up alone. I had always been so willing for that.

Paris answered me that she liked the idea of the Cuban's book. She liked the subject matter.

We pull up to my client's ranch house. The first time I came to meet her I was frightened. The house is dark and there are no windows, and I felt I was going into a cavern. I thought it a leftover homage to her drug days. I feared I was going into a den. But she turned out to be a person who means whatever she says, and she is generous of spirit, as is her husband.

She had been sexually abused, a drug addict, hooked for money, homeless, poverty stricken, all of it, only to meet a Bulgarian doctor in the Dominican Republican and her whole life changed to one of success and love. With its up and downs, but a steady drive toward the light. She, of course, credits God and prayer for anything good that has happened to her.

These are not people, like some I know, who are constantly unhappy. Quite the opposite. It is interesting how happiness is a gift of nature. Some people have it and some do not. It is not just an issue of your childhood. It is an issue of your attitude, which I think is just a blessing, to use her language.

I came to the door, and I could hear Donovan singing inside. I didn't think she was old enough. That's your lot in life, Lalania. I can't blame you, Lalania.

I was away from Kurt and Skene and even Sir Leo, with whom I had played tennis before I left. I am getting better so I am more willing to run around, and I saw he is not but that's his lot in life now. I can't blame him. Still, he was smiling and having a good time and joked about his copying Federer's return.

"At your age, bloke," someone yelled out, "Federer might have been copying your return."

She came to the door, happy to see me. You share so much when you write a book with someone. She never asks me about myself, and I find something attractive about that. We are not pretending to socialize, be friends. I don't like to socialize when I work. I just like to work. It is simple and efficacious.

She went into the kitchen to make some tea for us, and I realized if Irene fails me, I will still have landed somewhere new.

Because any action lands us somewhere new.

The Cuban woman has a raspy voice left over from years of drug use and I find it hard to understand her at times. She speaks rapidly, as people do in Spanish, even though she is speaking English with me. I focus, focus. She speaks of forgiving her husband's almost infidelity. She speaks of how she has a million followers on her radio show. She speaks of how she has made something of herself. We are in the business now of giving the book an upbeat ending.

Once we finished working, she showed me my room and Skene and I had a Zoom. It was quite late his time, but I wanted to connect with the island. Make sure it was still there and hadn't run away.

He looked like some kind of sea animal on the screen. It was like talking to a friendly porpoise, not so much in looks but in aspect. He was smiling when I made my little jokes, but he told me of having gone to some town to help a doctor out, one who was out ill and had a full load. He told me of going down to The Cavalier with an old friend and it felt quite celebratory. Everyone asked where I was, and he said who knows. I had gone off onto the mainland. Once they've seen Paris, Skene, they warned him, etcetera.

It was sort of fun and then I was tired, and he must have been so, too, and we said good night quickly, goodbyes always so awkward unless you are a real couple where it is not necessary to say you'll be in touch; it is a given.

He did not ask me about my return, which was an improvement. "We'll talk," I said, uncommitted.

"Good," he said.

I went back into the Cuban woman's living room, and we watched her radio show where she speaks of prayer and God with such passion. She breaks her speech up with some slight swaying of her body to pop songs and then recites a religious poem she has written to the pop music. The poems are quite good, and it is because she seems so sure of what she feels.

Another Lucia, although Lucia is busy making biblical talks on YouTube. Lucia with her obvious intelligence and kindness. The Cuban woman said there are a lot of people like herself out there. "Through our prayers," she said, "we are changing things."

In my work, people talk all the time about being "a writer," like it is some magical status. They will be real to themselves, they believe, if they are writers. They will have meaning. They all believe they are helping other people. "My writing," they call it. I personally would never put a possessive in front of the noun.

The Cuban woman, conversely, does not in the least talk about writing, even though I am the one doing the writing, and actually her music lyrics are quite good. She on the other hand is preoccupied with becoming a saint. I try to understand this. Lucia too, in her conversations on YouTube, seems to believe she is a person of religious personage.

Is death so terrifying that we are shoring ourselves up like this?

I suppose it is. But life shows there are only a few born to immortality. Shakespeare, others, Churchill, Stalin, St. Valentine, Freud, and Lucian Freud. Fewer and fewer of the standards will remain, as cultures discard what was once of value for the new.

The sands of time shift, and maybe we love dogs so much because they love without being bothered about any of this.

Chapter Fifty-Four

After I finished with Miami, Irene in Paris wanted me to do an interview in New York so, expensive as it was, I decided to fly there, rather than go back to England. This was all, in truth, over my head financially, but if all these books were coming out, and the publisher was risking all on them, then I should do the same.

The flight was very late, which is annoying but so be it. There I was in an airport working as I have been doing for years. I realized I read so much in my youth because in the old days all you could do in an airport was read. There were no laptops, no phones. Now I don't pull out my book. The one I have on me has not captured me, which may be part of the reason. Another book that was given to me. Sometimes I hate the books given to me. They take time from me, and they don't feel rewarding and yet I stay with the book because I suspect there must be something in there to have been given the book in the first place so I continue reading to encounter what it was the giver thought I would love. But often it doesn't happen.

And then I feel I have wasted time, of which we have so little.

If I do not have a book I love, I end up looking at the news. After all, it is written nowadays as consummate theater. It is written to incite and sadly there is something illusorily urgent in that. So I spend time getting annoyed.

Giving someone a bad book is almost a travesty, now that I think about it.

* * *

I sat on the floor of the airport since all the seats were taken with annoyed people and I waited for my trip to New York. I will visit my apartment, visit my landlord, visit my life there. Have I recovered from whatever drove me so away in the first place?

Maybe these spiritual people have made me more at ease about all of it.

The Waw now inside me, not out there; Lucia, my client, Skene, George, Sir Leo, the walks by the water, the Palace of Books Tennis Club replenished me.

It turned out the flight to New York was five hours late because someone went mad on the incoming plane. The airliine, unable to give a straight answer about takeoff, first said they will send in medical help and then the flight will go, second there must be protection against lawsuits then it will go, third there will be the police then it will go, and so on and so on, and no decision got made so no departure time was announced except for "it will go soon" and thus nobody could transfer flights. I found myself riled up, back in the game.

Once I got to my place, my old apartment seemed even older than before, not because of the building, England is much older, of course, but because it overflowed with the old me, the old me I was tired of. Before I fell asleep, I read a book review of a Graham Greene bio. He claimed he was bipolar, and aside from having sex with everyone and anyone, perhaps this is the writer's lot, the writer's curiosity, the writer's need to relax, can I please forget myself because my head, my head is always churning. It turned out he did everything he could—women, travel, drink—to run from himself. He used even religion, although these distractions were all short-lived. He did manage to see the world, and not as an Englishman but as one of the people. He could also run three plots at a time in one book. Fire and fury.

I fell asleep exhausted just reading about him. The next morning, I woke depleted, like I had been through a ring cycle that was not Wagner's. Although I have never listened to the whole ring cycle, which might also be a ring cycle.

These books of mine looked more and more like they were coming out in Paris, and now the discussion was around PR. I heard them talk talk talk of social media and inside I recoiled. "You are wrong, you are wrong," they said. "Stay open."

"I am not Cardi B," I replied.

"No, no," everyone said, "believe in the possibility of it. It can do amazing things."

"Like what?" I asked. "If one has all these followers, it does not mean they will buy books, it means they want you to follow them, so you'll buy their wares. I think it is fine for underwear and such things."

The publisher and PR agent looked at me sorrowfully.

And they should because this is the part of my work I detest. Making yourself a commodity. Today we were to have a live interview on TV (social media TV, let me add) and the publisher has been preparing as if it is a big event, whereas I believe no one will watch. I have hardly had time to consider it. It occurred to me that I had returned to the world, and it occurred to me I was once again at odds.

Stop it, I told myself. This is today, this is evolution, I told myself. Go with it. Learn. It is just your fear. I am always having someone show me on their phone their interviews and broadcasts and if God said curiosity is a sin, as my Miami client told me, there is no danger of curiosity in this world about the other. All our eyes are glued to ourselves on screens.

I prepared for a tiny cocktail party this evening that I was giving for my kind and beautiful New York landlady. I have been blessed with kind and beautiful landladies, there and here. Perhaps they are a salve from God for not having a mother, they provide a home. I answered a whelm of mail. I edited and tomorrow I would meet my US agent who more wants to be friends than be an agent for me since she likes to tell me, "You are not commercial," and the guillotine comes down.

What we usually do is discuss her lack of love life and the self-publishing business she has started. That is how much she believes in commercial publishing.

Then she looks at me as if I am mad since I have nothing to add to the subject of commercial acumen. Instead, I lift my coffee to my lips and steadfastly believe if you build it, they will come.

New York was cold and unbelievably Graham Greene only wrote five hundred words a day and produced all that work. The laurels go to the hare, evidently, I thought, as I put the hors d'oeuvres out.

Then I waited. I told myself part of being human is to be able to go with flux. Nomads have this skill. The flux of windstorms. The flux of dried-up oases. The flux of powerful tribes that become a dying-out tribe. Nothing is stable. The dunes ebb. One continues riding one's camels through it, with goodwill and seriousness about one's work.

As I looked out the window, I saw the city rushing, making and spending money. It is the currency of life here. There is a pulsing, which one can hook into.

I realized Skene was right. I am being pulled back. Where he is and I was, there is no pulse except the inner one. Sir Leo hears the pulse in his mind's ear as he plays.

Whereas in the city, the pulse is integral to survival.

Yes, this culture creates Kurts and their jumping-on little fish for their own profit.

And yes, there is almost no time here to do real work that is not about profit. I had taken to writing in cabs to and from meetings. The inner life shoved into corners to and from commerce.

The anxiety of the tension here passes as the current of life. And then one's life is over. And was that current important? Was entertaining ourselves important? TV shows. Films. Ads, constant ads. Voices everywhere talking about what is happening. New restaurants. New movies. Everyone reaching out to be fed more. More commentary. More assistance.

The still small voice, often not heard.

And then there are those like Sir Leo and Lucia and Skene who are inside themselves, like mystics.

And we admire them, but most of us don't become them.

Chapter Fifty-Five

Two days later I got on a plane for Paris.

I visited Irene and saw various pictures of me on her office wall, as art. She was choosing between them for marketing materials, and I looked at myself as if I were someone I didn't know. There was a watchfulness in my eyes in all the photos. I turned away to study Irene instead. She was wearing her signature beret inside her home, her glasses sliding down her aquiline nose. She had an open-neck sweater on, showing cleavage, which is not quite American, but it is her long red hair and swan neck where the eye travels.

She said, "Good, you are here. We have a sound check in less than two hours for a program where they will be discussing your books."

I tensed immediately.

She saw it and said, "It's just a sound check. The show is tomorrow."

As if that were any relief.

I looked round her office and there were copies of another book of mine she brought out many years ago. Someone will have to throw these out when she or I die.

I wanted to tell her again that I spoke with a friend before I left, and we both agreed that social media may not be all it is cracked up to be if you are doing something other than giving makeup tricks. But I knew Irene did not want to hear this. She continued to believe in it. I wonder why? I told myself it is her own desire to have the ethers do the work.

I am old-fashioned and think work is slugging away.

Instead, I complimented her on how good everything looked, which it did. And that was all her vision.

Even this confounded thing of six books. Who can review six books of an unknown author?

I had that thought when she had brought up the idea of a collection but somehow just got caught up in the creativity of the whole thing. And no doubt my vanity acted as an anesthesia to clear thinking.

Woody Herman played on her stereo.

"How is it going with Skene?" she asked.

"I am a bit indolent. Maybe he is, too."

"Why?"

"I don't know. Maybe I don't want to live there forever. Too isolated."

"You could go back and forth. It seems he has the money for that."

"I don't know—I need more vibrancy. I went there as a kind of salve to a broken heart."

She looked at me. "Well, I was thinking," she said, "that you know how in the last book you meet a man called Bill, right?"

"Yes."

"I think that is going to happen. He suits you."

I laughed. "That would be nice." Then I added, "Someone had to die in the book for that to happen."

"Maybe something in you has to die, and then it will happen."

"Perhaps." I smiled.

We talked about the PR proposal and this and that, and then I followed her to her kitchen, where she began preparing dinner for her husband.

"Want to stay?"

I get kind of bored having dinner at people's houses. "I think I'll walk around and find a jazz club somewhere."

Woody had reminded me of the joys.

"I'll wait for JP to come home, and he can tell me where to go," I said.

And then we just chatted about this and that, other writers she was bringing out, and the state of her own books.

Later that night, in a warm and quiet club, I sat and listened to the man's fingers dancing on the bass. Now the drummer coming in, and then the horns. In New York, they would have all applauded wildly here, the jumping of the horns, but in Paris, they are quiet, religious about it all, as the drummer now does his solo and then the musicians all blow out an ending.

Polite applause.

Just as I was wondering about that, Leon Thomas came on to sing. The mood tempered down to sultry. He began: "There was a time when peace was on the earth and joy and happiness would reign and each man knew his worth."

I almost wanted to cry. Peace and Happiness for every man. It was why I left originally. I wanted to focus on finding happiness for every man.

I was in the no man's land of music. As I listened, I decided I could only stay on that British island if I opened a jazz club. Maybe I should. I would meet a musician and fall in love. And he would be like a sailor who came back now and then to me.

Then the singer went on to talk about how awful New York is. "Plenty of rats and roaches, so get in line. They got enough welfare for everyone."

This man sang of his experiences, I could tell. Songs of oneself. What I admire.

Chapter Fifty-Six

Two days later, I was on the island. As I took the ferry across, I was again struck at the peace and the sea and the sounds of birds and the soft light. Now I felt I couldn't leave it. It was as if, when I was there, something in me cleaved. My being quieted down. I arrived at the dock and George came out of his coffee shop.

"I've found a better coffee for you," he said. "Juan Valdez or something. Come have one. I want to hear what's going on."

Excellent idea, and it was good to see George.

The coffee was indeed delicious, and I complimented him.

"Made with loving care," he said proudly. "I even got you these almond biscuits because they're the only thing you eat ravenously."

"That is so lovely of you," I replied.

"Yes, it is," he agreed, and sat down. "Now, what's going on?"

"In New York, you would be called a yenta."

"A busybody, aye?" he asked.

I nodded. "Nothing's going on. But I am a bit delighted to see how happy I am to be back here. I had thought maybe I was too urban."

"You've only been here a few hours. We'll see what happens in two days."

"True, but this morning it all seems so pristine. So untouched by what is sullied."

"Yes, the problems of life here are a bit normal, unlike other places. No mass murders."

"No."

"Are you going to see Skene?"

"Why are you so interested about Skene?" I asked.

"Because I think you're both intelligent and good people and shouldn't be alone. That he would give you the freedom you need, and you would give him the same and you could have a pleasant life rather than live in a hovel by yourself, walking around foraging coffee and the odd drink with Sir Leo. I think you would experience things you haven't before. Safety. And a home. And someone who supported you in whatever it is you gad about doing. I think you would make him laugh, like you make me laugh, and rather than him buying paintings, he might be content looking at you."

"What's wrong with paintings?"

"Nothing, but you could look at them together. There's art in the moment, you know."

"George, you are the oddest person."

"I am not in the least," he said. "I think I'll try this coffee, too." He poured himself a cup and put some milk in it and then sipped it, questioningly. "Marvelous," he said.

"How could I give this up for Skene's coffee?" I asked.

"I could teach him."

"Wouldn't come with such salient lectures."

"You can still come here for the almond biscuits."

The sun was out, and it was a bit warm. "Let's go stand outside and take in the sun a bit," I said.

We opened the door and there were some large stones near his coffee shop, so we sat on those and just looked out at the harbor sipping our coffee.

"I've looked at this view all my life," he said, "and it never gets boring. It's infinitely interesting and changing and restoring. All my life. I think people leave here because the people get boring to them. No challenges, but there are, there are. Do you find life better in the big city?"

"Well, it's more differentiated. You know, big things go on and people feel big being around big things, I guess."

"But"—he nodded to the harbor—"is that a small thing?"

"No."

"So let Skene help you. It will do him good, too, to help someone."

"Well, he does help people."

"All the better," George said, standing up, ending the conversation.

"Really, you should have been a psychoanalyst."

"No. I've been doing all the talking. I'd simply hate it if you had been."

"You have a point."

I trudged up the hill and Lucia came out and walked down toward me, her red hair, as usual, flying.

"So much has gone on," she said. We were in the garden next to my little hut.

"Really?"

"Yes, I will tell you about it. Welcome back. I put a heater in your place. Do you want something to eat?"

"No, thanks. I just came from George. You do know your ex-husband is living on this island?"

She smiled like a girl, and I once again remarked to myself how youthful her face is. "Of course, I know," she said, laughing. "I also know he's doing well health-wise and mind-wise. As am I. Well, I am losing my sight a bit. I have to have these shots in the eye. You can't feel them, but the thought is so awful. It staves off the blindness."

"Terrible," I said, "but good you have the shot."

"I wish I didn't have to go into the town for them. I have been promised my sight restored. But maybe God means something else."

"Must have been nice being married to Sir Leo. He's so interesting and passionate," I said. "Probably was great looking, like you."

She thought for a minute. "Yes, I agree. He was."

"And all the music—"

She looked out at the harbor. "Oh, I never liked music that much. I didn't understand it. Or have the patience for it. That was one of our problems, deep down. Who knows? Maybe we made a mistake divorcing, although I got on better with my second husband. But I loved Tanek much more deeply. Maybe it was young love."

"Why do you not see each other now?"

She turned to me and suddenly we were like people who had always known each other. She looked deeply into my eyes. "It's too painful that we can't have what we once had back then," she said, simply.

"Why can't you?"

"When you're young, you're creating something together. Older. I don't know." And she turned to look out at the sea.

I suddenly thought she wanted to be with him.

"Why is it you both ended up here if not something going on?" I asked. I turned my face to the sun for the warmth, and, as I did so, the sun made me feel as if I had all the time in the world.

"Yes, in that way he and I are alike," she said. "In a deep, deep way. I think it's enough we're both here. We both know we're here. It's like we're together, we have not forgotten each other or abandoned each other but understand our lives moved on. Yet we know we're both here, as if just our souls being near each other is comforting."

"I find this sad," I said, "like you both haven't the courage . . ."

"No, we hurt each other deeply, as young people can, and doing that we needed to stay separate. I suppose we both can't forgive ourselves and that, dear, is all right. Don't be upset. Not all life is simple. You know that. The heart in conflict with itself and all that . . ."

"Faulkner said that," I said.

"Who?" she asked.

"A writer, in his Nobel Prize speech."

"Well, it's not that unusual a thought," she said.

"It's unusual wording."

"Well, I don't know." Here she got flustered. "What about you and Skene?"

"Why do you all ask that?"

She said nothing, waiting for a response.

"My heart is in conflict with itself," I said, squinting a bit.

"Why? You mean over that man who visited you?"

"No, not really."

"Your heart is in conflict," she said, "about moving forward."

As she said it, I knew it was true. Why am I always so recalcitrant? "Yours is in conflict about moving backward and mine is in conflict about moving forward," I said.

"God will work it out."

I nodded because I didn't know what else to say.

"He brought you here," she added.

"Something did."

"You had a vision. The vision will lead you. You'll see."

And with that, she put her hand on my arm, then turned and went back to her house.

Chapter Fifty-Seven

I was still working on that play for the woman in Philadelphia where God is a character who saves the day. She is the one who has three sons who went to jail and everything else that could go wrong. Now she helps everyone she knows.

I who never go to any church have three people in my life who talk God all the time.

Skene had once said he realized if he were younger, he would be much more aggressive about moving things forward with us; in other words, impatient and conjuring up plots and ways to make me do what he wanted. Now he just goes with the flow.

"That is one of the few good things about aging; things are less cataclysmic," I had said.

Skene did not know I was back since I had decided to return on a whim. I had not called. I decided to walk over to his house. I was not sure what was going to happen between Skene and me. I just liked being with him, felt good with him, but, if he were a character in a book I was writing, this might be the time to kill him off since what else to do with him? What others might call a deus ex machina, speaking of God. But I don't think death is the solution to us.

It was warm out and it was a most lovely walk, with the scent of sea roses as I swung along.

I got to his place and felt sad there was no George the dog to invite me in. George the dog had died recently, Skene had mentioned that on a Skype while I was away, and I was sure

Skene was grieving. Even I missed George as I came up to the house, his intense interest in my arrival and how I fit in.

Skene should get another dog, I thought. I had seen one evening a ghost dog when I was walking, all white and long legs, and those blue eyes. I had been bewitched by the dog's beauty. I had gone to him, and he jumped up onto me. I had to keep walking, but that dog stayed inside me the whole way. I could conjure him even now. Dogs don't leave you.

I knocked on the door. Skene did not answer quickly as Sir Leo would. I must go see Sir Leo too this week.

Maybe Skene was not home.

Suddenly he came round the side of the house, holding shears in one hand. "Oh, I was just doing some gardening. I didn't hear you. Isn't that funny that I came round just now? It's like love stories. You know, how they always run into each other, even if they're in another country."

As he spoke, he was looking me over, dare I say, appreciatively.

I laughed.

"It's beautiful today, isn't it?" he said.

"Yes, very." I was smiling, as was he.

"It's good to see you back. Do you want to sit down in the garden?"

"Yes, I never saw it in daylight."

We walked round the house and I was surprised to see a fountain, an abstract of the three Graces, which he must have bought on one of his expeditions, looking for art. It was situated in the middle like we were in Rome, and it was surrounded by peonies, lots of peonies.

There was also a section in his garden of just trees.

"I could walk you round my fruit trees—but another time, perhaps. They will just make me see what I should be tending."

Tending, I thought.

We sat in some garden chairs, the sun warming me.

"Did you have a good trip?" he asked.

"I did. I discover I like both lives. They suit each other."

"Like a couple," he said.

"I suppose."

"Ever enthusiastic," he said, laughing.

I smiled.

"Of course, I can't figure out how to put both lives together," I said.

"From the outside, it looks like you are doing so."

"I should have been born rich like you," I said. "I suit the lifestyle."

"Again, looking from the outside, it seems you have been born rich."

"Yes," I agreed, because I felt rich with the garden, the sun, walking, and the moment.

I closed my eyes and took in the garden. "Wow, even the sounds of the trees and the air are exquisite."

I looked at him, and he was puzzling over something.

"What is it?" I asked.

"Methinks you're always wrestling because you can't give yourself what you want."

"Lucia said almost the same thing. Maybe I fear if I come here more often, I will let go of the city."

"People do," he said. "I've seen it many times. They don't die of it."

I looked out at the sea roses bordering his land with another house and thought the city doesn't have borders. It overflows with everything.

But then I looked at him sort of inspecting the steps to an outdoor office he had at the back of the garden, and I also thought, You can open a door, darling. You don't have to be on the outside looking in. Was I the man looking through the window at myself?

I stood up. "You should get another dog," I said.

"I know, I think I will."

Chapter Fifty-Eight

"I keep trying to listen to Vaughan Williams but I am on hold with this place to fix my computer and they play that awful tinny music," Sir Leo said, when I dropped by. He was on the phone. "It's a plot to drive us all mad."

Indeed.

Chapter Fifty-Nine

Something has happened without my doing.

Yesterday afternoon, I switched from classical music on Lucia's radio to what turned out to be Aretha Franklin. It is true I live in a box, but it was almost like being in one of those cages where you dance for men except I was dancing for myself. I had a fiesta, this station played a number of her songs, and I just danced madly and sang along with the words, imagining the backup singers as two friends of mine whom I have not seen in years. I had no feeling of time, although I was supposed to go to Skene's to watch another film. But I could not tear myself away from the dancing and the imagining of singing each line, one at a time to Kurt's son and then his wife, for some reason, even Kurt, who sat back and watched amazed I could sing like this, and then I moved on to singing lines to lovers I'd had and lovers I wished I'd had and even Skene was there listening to me singing and he got, only by mathematics of the lines, "Baby I love you I love you I love you I love you Baby I love you."

It was interesting to me that I learned, through one of Aretha's songs, that there is the drive in all our female subconscious for the man who will bring the nomad out in us. "He's the kind of guy that would say hey, baby, let's get away, let's go some place, where, I don't care."

I had always felt the right man gave you love but also keys to inner and outer road trips. It would be amazingly beautiful if he could show you a part of the desert you did not know, a part of the desert that takes you to a new oasis in yourself that possibly could change your life for the better.

This clarity as I danced around was as if I had found a pot of gold. I hoped Lucia could not see me moving so passionately round my place, but then she probably is dancing with God up there and if she isn't, she is a woman too, and she would understand, undoubtedly.

Then I decided to walk to Skene's but took a long route since I was dancing so much inside. I began planning a birthday party for myself where I turn an august age and I would invite all my students, everyone I knew and cared about, to a major party. Young people, old people, children, and the music would have everyone free and getting on together in joy. I had to elongate my walk to Skene's to further enjoy this party in my mind. I was a bit confused as to where this party would be held and how I could mix babies into the dancing but of course the toddlers could run around and dance too and friends who rarely smile now would smile easily and there would be such well-being, such appreciation of life, such unity. It was all so enjoyable that I could not knock on his door.

I turned around and went to one of the stone pillars and sat there, one where the strange man had been who had given me the glass heart.

My heart right now was not glass, it was pulsing with love, but that strange gift was, I was sure, part of this pulsing.

I will invite that man to the mega dance party.

Where was all this joy coming from? I was beside myself. We all have heard that artists tend to the bipolar, and this felt a bit like it, I could hardly contain this bustling dance party inside me, although I pride myself on equanimity but looking at myself sitting on this stone in a place so far from my home did not speak, one might say, of a flair for equanimity.

You could say this dance party was control on my part. Here it was, being held in my head, with the music I am picking and the responses all the guests were having, so witty and loving they were, and having such a wonderful time; sadly, this was indeed my party, not theirs.

At that, I jumped off the stone pillar and headed to Skene's.

He didn't seem to notice I was late and opened a bottle of white wine. I had brought nuts, and he tried the wine and said it was off. Then he opened a red wine that he didn't like that much either but we both decided was bearable and we chatted about this and that. I explained my late arrival to Aretha Franklin, and then we sat down to *Sweet Smell of Success*. A gritty New York movie in black and white. The acting superb. The script, to me, taking advantage of drama so much that it seemed a bit mad, but that was the point, and I saw I have trouble believing people can be thoroughly despicable. Black and white emotions. Surely, they break into the grey.

I was so tired now that I rested my head on the arm of his couch and put my legs on the couch. He looked over and seemed delighted that I was doing something trusting. His delight frightened me a bit, but I decided not to jump away.

He put his hand on my bare foot and began rubbing it.

It felt so intimate. I might fall through the couch.

After the film ended, we went upstairs. I decided to sleep over. I had said I was going to try dancing with someone, letting them hold me.

When we were in bed, he kissed my right breast, and I, who had begun to think I cannot feel anything erotic anymore, felt desire come up in my body. We ended up making love and I found myself responding, occasionally retreating into my own mind and all its tangents, but often being there with him erotically. It was new for me. Kurt had not known how to reach that part of me. Skene made this intimacy seem normal and I woke the next morning, knowing I had crossed over somewhere new again.

When I got up, I felt a strange wholeness, fulsomeness. I had joined not only with him but with my own body.

I got back to my place and sent emails to friends that were full of witticisms or nitwitticisms, and I even had two ideas for things I wanted to write, if I could. That didn't mean those ideas would last. Ideas are like flowers. They can prematurely wilt or, if one is lucky, bloom.

But deep inside me, that excitement was still there.

I decided to take a break, and, as I walked to George's coffee shop, feeling full and enthusiastic at the day, I thought, I have remembered what it is to be happy. It is possible for me. I must take hold of it somehow.

And, as I walked into George's, I could not believe it.

"What?" George said.

"You're playing King Pleasure."

"I know that," he said. "I love the way he sings, don't you?"

"Absolutely. It's wild to hear it here."

"You think we are backwater here, do you?"

"Not at all." I laughed. "But I am a bit surprised."

"Why should you and Sir Leo be the only ones having all the fun?"

"You are absolutely right," I said, smiling, and left with my takeaway coffee that he so mocks but always has ready for me.

Chapter Sixty

I returned to New York because I had to. It had to do with that play for the woman in Philadelphia. I had to act it out with her because people cannot always read plays. They can't follow them.

Once I landed, we were held on the tarmac quite far away from the terminals and when I looked out the plane window, I saw troops. Our plane slowly taxied to a spot on the runway and then came to a full stop, but it was not close to a gate. We were told we would be taken to the airport in buses and indeed they were lined up outside the plane window, in this no man's land of arrivals. This busing to a gate is unusual for a transatlantic flight. Usually, you dock right into the airport itself. But when we walked down the ramp off the plane, the buses weren't going at all, and we were told to have lunch outside near the plane. There were tables set up and a buffet delivered from those little food buses that usually stock the planes' pantries.

The troops all had rifles, ah, back in the USA, and maybe, I thought, these are not troops at all. The "soldiers" seemed angry, and I wondered if there had been a coup of some sort. There has been such anger in what is my country. One side was for freedom, believing the other side was for repression under the umbrella of equality and caring. The freedom people were considered off their rockers and conspiracy theorists. "This is politics, this is politics," Kurt used to say in the old days when we were still a couple. "Don't get so upset."

Why not? I thought, looking around. Something was changing in the States. Every voice was either now talking about what had gone wrong, or afraid to say that things had gone wrong. It all depended on what news they read. Whom they believed. I believed the news itself was the cause of what had gone wrong. Screaming. Screaming. Vilifying. Choosing who they wanted and only reporting on what aided that person. The other side, the news would say, is bad. Few spoke about what had gone right in this country and yet so much had gone right in this country. On the backs of others, yes, but then there were so many who died fighting for the backs of others. I was thoroughly confused by what I heard and by my own sadness.

It was eerie having lunch outside a plane with troops standing by. I would have expected this in the Sudan or somewhere, not in New York.

It made me feel ill. I did not want to talk about it with the other passengers but of course that was impossible. As I helped myself to lunch, which was surprisingly well put out and abundant and I thought this too is America, I asked the person next to me, a man wearing a tie but no jacket, someone who might be in middle management, "What do you think is going on?" I ladled some food onto a cardboard plate. I have noticed I am always hungry in transit even though I do nothing physical. Hunger grounding me.

The answers, as I listened to disparate people, about what was going on were all over the place and they traveled along party lines. Some talked about who owed whom what and how is liberty defined and are we going socialist because we have so many have-nots and some rich said, "Okay, take the bulk of my money, I get it," and someone else said, "Hey, I worked hard for what I have," and there were many reasons, and whatever one side said, the other said the same in different language, everyone accusing each other of what they themselves did, and now I saw it had come to troops on the tarmac.

Is this a war I want to fight?

It wasn't my war, it was the media's, and now it was being actualized. I had been poor all my life and worked. I had tried like everyone else to live a decent life, as I suspect is true for most people. Anger and revenge were never on the agenda.

I put my hands to my ears and went and sat alone at a table and waited.

Finally, we were put on the buses and sent through customs, as if things were normal, and no mention was made of the "troops."

It occurred to me that that might be because somewhere it had become normal.

When I finally got to my New York apartment and put on Brahms and a pavane to quiet me down, I realized I needed live jazz. To me, it spoke far better than the soldiers of what should be protected. I walked downtown to a club I had gone to many times. One could almost say I had grown up in jazz clubs. An eighteen-year-old girl walking down the soggy steps to a pulsing and rushing that I took to, like heroin, and was forevermore after. When in doubt, a jazz club.

On the stage I saw a white piano player, Black horn players and drummers, an Asian bassist, one Sikh on the organ. How it should be.

They were all smiling at one another, to themselves and to their hands and fingers. This is how it should be.

And my heart was smiling at them.

I ordered a drink and that was as good as it gets, a drink and this music. Things were sorting themselves out.

And then I saw Kurt. Naturally, he was with a woman. Both dressed swankily. He was not with Mrs. Shapiro's orphan but that was not exactly a surprise to me.

He caught my eye. People know when they are being watched.

I did not nod. Just looked at him and then at the stage.

How I had once loved that man.

At the intermission, he came up to me.

"You should smile more," he said, standing over me, smirking.

That incensed me. "I am not an idiot who has to go around smiling for no reason. I am not on camera all the time, like some people."

He was quiet for a minute, confused. He probably thought he'd said something interesting.

I wanted to punch him.

"I see you've returned," he said.

I didn't reply.

"Well, I also see you're being rude," he added, and I nodded, and then, in a huff, he returned to his seat.

I listened to the love songs being played and thought, What does he expect? He was attacking me and all I had done was not extend friendship after he had insulted me when he came to England and went off with another woman, as if he was pulling something off on me. Was it some legal trick he'd learned in school to make the other person guilty ("you are not smiling," like I am a baboon), make the other person feel guilty no matter what is going on?

Here I was once again, craving kindness.

Here I was once again, feeling alone.

Yes, yes I had the music, but all of a sudden the heaviness of being alone became such a burden that I could hardly feel or hear. I just wanted to go lie down and not get up.

I had done this to myself. It was my fault.

I had not let anyone touch me.

I looked at Kurt and he was not touching that woman. Nor she him.

When he'd tried to touch me so awkwardly, in those years, I would pull away.

"See what you do? You pull away when I touch you. This is what people do," he'd say to me, as he tried to touch me like an awkward teenager.

Really? I thought. I hated it.

That is why I felt there was nowhere for me to go but to some end somewhere.

And when I ran away, I did not know there would be people there wanting to touch me with their hearts, not artifice, and touch me gently.

Kurt had ruined the safety I felt at the jazz club so I got up, put my coat on, and walked out into the night. My phone sent me a request from some website to learn more about the criminals around me. This is how people think now. Not about what is criminal in ourselves.

The streets felt good, the action, but I felt the weight of it all. I didn't want to fly away right now but I did want to be braver in love.

Chapter Sixty-One

I started going back to the English sea town more and more often. What happened was that when I felt a bit lost, when I felt that I had had too much of everyone castigating the other, taking pride in calling out the other, like we are Stasi, when it got to a certain point, I would book a flight.

I didn't think about money. Paris postponed their delivery date of my books, overwhelmed with the task of putting six out at once, and this was not surprising.

The books had been postponed a lifetime anyway.

Once I arrived, I would land and take a train to the promontory.

But first, first I would stand where I originally stood, and fasten my eyes on the silver steeple across the harbor. I would just stand and take in the town's light, how it bounced out, as if onto me, its silver light acting as a magnetic agency cleaning out all that seemed unimportant.

I stood there and let it travel through my body so I could go to those places where the best of myself could maybe come alive.

I was also looking forward to the quiet talks, of the moment, when seeing Sir Leo, George, Lucia, and even Skene.

But mostly I was excited for the quiet of the walks.

The people, it must be noted, seemed older here. Had I moved into that country of old people? The media seemed to be pushing me away and toward them.

It didn't seem like me to accept that fate gracefully.

I was now on the ferry to the high road and thought, No, I am not relegating myself to that fate. I will just return here now and then to shore up my soul with that light but otherwise stay in the fray of life. And hope that I can communicate some of that silver light to others.

"Missed my beautiful face, did you?"

"Of course," I said as George poured me a coffee and gave me some fig bars. Funny how everyone had them here.

"What's been going on?" I asked, a little nervous that someone might have died.

"Nothing," he said. "That's why we're here. What's been going on out there?"

"Every second someone is accused of kissing someone's hand without the woman's permission or being a racist or not getting enough ratings and so on. Other than that, the same."

"Well, that's true everywhere," he said.

"I know. Complaining is an art form now. Even I've mastered it."

"Yes, watch out. What do you think of this coffee?"

"Excellent."

"I keep perfecting it," he said. "Gives me something to do."

"What is that Zen expression? Chop wood, carry water."

"Right," he said.

I went up the hill and Lucia, naturally, had left fresh flowers for me and a muffin, without my telling her I was coming. It amazed me, really. It's not possible she did that every day. Did she see the boat bring me over? That's possible.

I was still her tenant, I still had not decided where I belonged.

I chucked everything inside and even though I was tired I decided to go down to the Palace of Books Tennis Club. Might move around for an hour. I had been sitting for almost twenty-four hours.

I had my own racquet now, not that it made much difference, but it is a small commitment.

As I walked, I could hear Verdi's Requiem in my mind, which made me a bit nervous. I wondered if Sir Leo liked that piece. Hard to imagine someone not loving it.

I suddenly realized that, as I had looked at the steeples, I had not looked down for the dead fishermen. I had forgotten to.

I went in and the Asian woman said hello as if this was just another day, and it is.

"I need a partner," I said.

She picked a tall slender woman who had lovely manners, and I was a bit frightened since now I realized I was tired.

I also knew I would forget that fact on the court and that was why I came here.

I looked out the window, as the other woman got ready, and the sky was an almost purple blue, and the steeple was closer here and I could see it had the wrong time on it.

"Why is it called the Palace of Books Tennis club?" I asked the Asian woman before I made my way to the court.

"Everybody asks but no one knows."

"Do you think it was a library before?"

She looked at me. "I don't know. No one has ever asked."

That amused me even more.

I played fairly well with the woman, tired as I was, and all felt good and I looked forward to a long quiet sleep in Lucia's little house. I had the feeling that in the deep silence I would be restored, just by being there.

Chapter Sixty-Two

In the morning, I was renewed, not perfect, but not dragging. It was a bright blue sunny day, contrary to all those tales of England being eternally grey, and it was a Thursday and I had some errands to run, even a hovel like this needs paying attention to, and, at four, I would go to Sir Leo's for my piano lesson. He would be most surprised.

He doesn't like the phone, and neither do I.

By 4 pm, I walked along the coastline and thought how nomads care more about water than any other aspect of their life in the desert. Sand, which all the young people used to go to dreamily stare at as if it were an ocean, can be the nomads' enemy since, in storms, it blinds or it brings about droughts, and I have to say, as I looked out over the sea, that I have the same obsession as the nomads. There must be water, only then do I feel safe. It both stills and moves me. If I am not by it, I am longing for it. Sometimes it feels like it is the real love.

Thank God, I thought, as I walked, that I had brought myself here, even if the whole thing was mad, my bank account losing sea level because of it. But my soul, my soul had needed this ocean and its particular light. I could have gone on an internal tangent about what is a soul anyway as I looked at everything on my way to Sir Leo, but, instead, I just walked, drinking in the smell of the sea and the sound of seagulls cawing out a fandango. Whenever I hear that kind of action, I wish I were wearing a swirling skirt and could begin swaying. Well, I was doing it inside.

The cypress trees bowed as I arrived.

I bowed back.

And the door opened.

"How did you know?" I asked.

"I may be old, but I am not blind."

I kissed him on the cheek, lord or not lord.

"Well," he said, "that should keep me going a bit longer."

"You have to keep going because I am getting acclimated to being here. We're both going to die, I know, but see if you can put it off."

"I'll do what I can. Speaking of that, I think you should leave that terrible place of Lucia's. This place is enormous. You can have a space here."

How could I tell him that physical space is irrelevant? I need the feeling of being free, and, in his house, I would not have it.

"I won't bother you," he said.

"I know, but I am a bit of a lone ranger."

"Well, that gets tiring, you know."

"I am well aware, but I am one anyway."

We had a lesson, or at least he played and I listened, Albinoni dances with occasional slower movements, which I always prefer, and then we had a drink and I took pleasure in hearing what was going on with him and music as I looked out his window at his fulsome garden and then I thought, I want to see Skene.

I left and began walking there. In truth, I liked the walking about as much as anything. I would just knock on his door. If he surprises me with a woman there, I will simply be polite.

Once again, he came round from the side.

"Do you actually live in the back?" I asked.

"No, I just am always wrestling with this garden and again I felt that someone was at the door. I must be turning into a dog, now that George has gone, and sense when someone is here."

That wouldn't be bad, I thought, I've always wanted a dog.

We went to sit in his garden and I updated him on the books (late, of course) and on my business slowing down to nonexistent, which was probably not too surprising given my current lifestyle, not exactly a nose-to-the-grindstone lifestyle, and I had not thought that age would be so pleasant, with how it graces you to be fully in the moment, and you stop worrying about everything and are so grateful for the moment . . . any moment, and now it was getting dusk. He had switched to a new clinic that he is committed to that is tending the underprivileged, as he put it.

I looked out at the sea. "You mean the nomads? The people who have moved here? The ones who have left their homes?"

"I don't know about nomads," he said. "But, yes, it's a veritable United Nations in the waiting room."

I still stared at the sea as the sun kept falling into it and thought, He is integrating. So wonderful. Or maybe I was.

"Let go down to The Cavalier," he said.

And I was grateful he said that, too. I am not the type to want to move toward pots and pans. I want to move.

We walked down, past the sea roses and other roses, and I remembered a student whose father gave her a rose he had himself grown as a gift when she graduated college; he gave her a lot more in life, financial freedom, but he gave her that rose and it was such a wonderful thing to me.

My father never got to see me graduate because I never did and for neither of us was there peace enough for a rose.

Skene and I didn't speak, and I found that spoke volumes, as usual.

I had never had that before, where I almost preferred silence with someone. It was almost like a language

* * *

Many people were there and plenty of chat going on around us, and Skene told me he'd found a new artist he likes, and he was thinking of putting a clinic in his house as well, at least for people round here; they came to him anyway, he said, but at least it would all be more set up and I encouraged it because as far as I am concerned any action is progress and I asked if he had ever been to Capri? No, he hadn't. I said I wanted to go, thinking he could afford it, and he said, "Okay, why don't we do it?"

That was simple, I thought. A rose.

After dinner, we walked back to his place together.

He unlocked the door, and I went in.

"I miss giving George a treat right now," he said.

"Yes."

He began switching off lights, and I followed him up the stairs.

His bedroom was full of paintings, naturally, landscapes and a few abstracts, and I looked out over the sea for the real painting, not that I could see the sea, but I could hear the fishing boats going out at night and I could see the lights on their masts, and, when I did, I caught a glimpse of the water.

"Beautiful here," I said.

"I agree."

I turned toward the bathroom.

"I got some more toothbrushes," he said.

"I thought the English don't care about teeth."

"This one is electric, so it appealed to me. I also got some other things for you."

I went to the extra bathroom, and, indeed, there were fresh toothbrushes, and now a face cream, not bad, a British brand I did not know but it looked somewhat expensive and a gentle face wash by the same brand. They stood on the counter, as if placed by a housekeeper in a five-star hotel.

I looked at myself in the mirror and thought this was all so much easier when I was twenty-two and had no idea what I was doing. I just wanted to be liked then.

I got into bed and told myself that my old body isn't that bad. It is agile from tennis, and I am somewhat slender, at least my clothing size appears as so.

I am soft.

I could tell I was trying not to be the ugly daughter that my mother ran from or the woman that Kurt would not look at.

If I were in bed with Kurt now, he would put a heavy leg over me, like a lock. It would repel me, and I would try to squiggle out of it.

"Why are you squirmy?" he would ask.

There was no lock right now. My body was free to move as it wanted.

"Are you all right?" Skene asked.

"Yes, you?"

He laughed. "You'd think we were teenagers doing it for the first time."

"It almost feels like that to me. It's so long since I've been in bed with someone who doesn't distance himself from me. It takes some getting used to."

"Your friend was like that?"

"He hardly ever touched me, and if he did, it was not erotic, it was disembodied, like he didn't want to. And he never looked at me during sex and he never kissed me. That about sums it up."

I felt sick as I said it.

"Is that what you were running from?"

"Maybe."

"I am so sorry," he said. "It almost sounds abusive."

"It was, but not intentionally. I thought he might be gay, but I think it was something else."

"I suppose it doesn't matter."

"That's what I came to, too."

He held my hand gently in bed and sweetly massaged my fingers and my hand.

"The unspoken question is, why did I put up with it and collude with it?" I said, into the night.

"Maybe you loved him."

"Yes. Maybe. "

"I think you're rather understanding of people. Not that judgmental."

"Maybe."

"I wouldn't be hard on yourself. Plenty of couples don't have sex at all. Or they beat each other up or whatever when they do have sex. We all think everyone is having some kind of perfect sex life but there is no such thing, probably."

I didn't want to ask him about his own experiences. There was time for all that.

"Maybe I should go more slowly with you," he said.

"I don't know what you should do. It's like a dance. One follows."

"Of course, you know the old joke about a boy being told about how people have sex and he asked, 'How do they keep from laughing?'"

"I've heard it," I said. "The boy has a point."

"Well," he turned to me and put his arms around me, and brought his lips near mine, "shall we have a laugh?"

He was being gentle and connective. The gentleness was the salve, no question.

And then he kissed me. And I decided to relax into it, and we just kissed. And I did feel my body start to go liquid and warm, and my young self suddenly emerged from out of nowhere.

We stopped kissing.

"Well, that part is definitely nice," he said. "And not that funny."

I smiled.

"Let's try again," he said, and one thing led to another, and particularly I loved that he kissed my breasts. Kurt had touched them as if he were supposed to, not as if they were tender, and it was what, I realized, I had longed for. The lovemaking with Skene was neither a porno film nor ice cold but kind of happy, a way of being happy together, getting close, I realized, a way to be close, and sink into the other. It was sort of opening up a door where behind could be eroticism and could be different ways of knowing each other, most of which I had forgotten but maybe I should be glad that, late in life, I had returned to being a virgin, frightened and curious, with so much before me.

Not like Mrs. Shapiro's adopted daughter who already saw lovemaking as a tender of exchange, but more like my getting to see it now as a tender way to exchange and open myself to him, the other.

After we finished making love, and I amazingly had an orgasm, just because there was such attention being paid, as Willy Loman would say, we fell asleep, silent as usual, but only because in that silence there was so much to be said that did not need to be.

Chapter Sixty-Three

Wwe had breakfast in his garden, and I must say there probably is nothing more pleasant than having coffee, even English coffee, over the sea in the sun with a man you might be allowing yourself to fall in love with.

I just sat there with the sun holding me and I remarked on my thought.

"Better if one adds in a dog," he said.

"Yes," I agreed.

Why had I waited so long for this? A simple pleasure that one truly needs. For centuries people have known this information. That it is good to be with someone you can trust who is kind to you on a summer morning. I had always chosen people who, like myself, had difficulties in giving themselves to beauty and trouble giving themselves to another. At least, I had done so in the last twenty years.

After a while, I said, "I better go home and change and generally pay some attention to my own life."

"All right," he said. And I loved that it was that simple. None of that Oh, stay, or Why? or Bring your things here. Just "All right."

"All right" was respectful.

I walked home and as I came up my hill there was Lucia, naturally, leaving my place. The one time I wished she weren't out.

But she just waved as she went to her house, and I opened the door to a raspberry muffin on my table.

I showered, changed, checked emails, and there were things to attend to. Irene wanted us to talk; I could tell she was struggling with this gargantuan project she had taken on. But I have juggled too much all my life, it is practically a lifestyle, and all I would be able to advise is to stay the course.

Once I had done all that, I sat outside in Lucia's garden. And there she was coming out toward me.

"I have never seen you sit in the garden," she said.

"I know. I am taking the day off."

"So good you are doing that." She pulled up a chair from the side of the messy garden and sat down next to me and was wearing a hat that had a flap over her eyes.

Actually, I had no work, which in itself was quite unusual and dangerous really, so what I was doing was taking the day off from worrying.

"How are your eyes?" I asked.

"God says I will get my sight back . . . so I believe."

I nodded.

We both looked out at the sea.

"I feel you won't be here too long, in my place," she said.

"Why is that?"

"I don't know. I just feel it."

"You think I will return to New York?"

"No. Sometimes you will, yes."

We were silent.

"Are you referring to Skene?" I asked.

"You managed to meet the two most important men here. Skene for his heart and soul and modesty, and Tanek for his life force and talent."

"Did you ever consider that he moved here because your husband had died and his wife had died? It is a bit coincidental, you've got to admit."

"Maybe," she said, laughing.

"Lucia," I said, "will you do me a favor?"

It was evening, cocktail hour here, and we were walking together toward Sir Leo's.

She was looking about under that hat with flaps over her eyes and I did not think she could see much; she held on to my hand or arm. She said, looking around probably with blurry vision, "This is the most beautiful walk, isn't it?"

She must be smelling the sea and hearing the trees.

"Are you going to live with Skene?" she asked.

"I don't know."

"Does he make you happy?"

"Yes. It is good to have someone whom you feel won't hurt you."

"Yes, your New York boyfriend did not desire you."

That cut a little quickly.

"I wonder what he did desire," I said.

Lucia said, "Perhaps to be left alone. Which you thought you wanted, too."

"Then why would he have come?"

"He liked that you desired him."

I thought that might be true and looked over at her again. She looked so lovely in the sunlight. Her red hair shining, and she had no lines on her face for an older woman, and such a beautiful smile. It moved me. She walked with force, and such trust of me as I guided her.

We were now at the cypress trees.

"How long since you've seen him?" I asked, as I held her hand more tightly. We were going into something new.

"A long time."

"You know how old he is?"

"Of course. But I am old, too."

"Actually, you will find that neither of you are," I replied.

Sir Leo opened the door and said, "Well, well, well." He was wearing an especially lovely cotton blue shirt and it was a pity she might not see it. He also had dark pants on, and he looked very regal.

"I brought you a surprise," I said.

"Hello, Lucia."

"Hello, Tanek."

"Come in. It's time for a cocktail," he said, laughing.

"That's why we're here," I said.

"You're both too disorganized to make one yourselves?" he asked.

"Precisely," I said.

He got busy tending. "Let's have something light. A pink champagne."

I laughed. He seemed happy.

"Lucia, you look well. Still beautiful."

"I agree," I said.

"And you, Tanek," she said, "you have not changed."

He laughed. "And you, who never used to lie."

She laughed, too. I loved their gaiety. They were communicating through that, and I thought, This is wonderful. I sat her down on a couch.

"I am so happy to see you," he said as he fussed round his silver tray after retrieving some pink champagne from his kitchen.

"I still believe you moved here because of her," I said. "It's a possibility, Sir Leo," I teased.

"These Americans are so boorish, aren't they?" he said to Lucia.

Lucia was smiling.

I should have brought Skene.

We chatted about his garden and my not having work, which they both felt was entirely uninteresting a topic and would change of itself and soon they got to some people in common and I stood up and said, "Well, I am going to leave you two for dinner. You two have much to talk about."

What I loved about Lucia was she did not try and talk me out of it. She understood.

"Don't you want a quick piano lesson?" he asked.

"Very funny."

"This young woman won't learn anything," he said to Lucia, then turned to me. "You don't even finish your tennis swing properly."

There was some truth to that.

"I do have a hard time doing things the right way," I said.

"But she does do things in the right way," Lucia said, coming to my defense. "She knows how to honor what is good. And now good is coming to her."

I scratched my nose. It did seem that way, although I could not tangibly say how. I was still broke. Would those books really come out? Would anything work, but I knew the thing was to keep going. Just to keep going. Even when I was suspicious of everything and sad about everything, to keep going.

I have a wonderful life, I thought. Full of excitement and creativity. It could not be better.

"I just changed my mind," I said to Sir Leo. "Play something before I go."

"What?"

"What did you love, Lucia?" I asked.

"She has terrible taste," he said.

"Well, you don't."

"I know," he said. "Since we're all in such a good mood how about Ravel's Mother Goose suite."

"Excellent!" I said.

"For four hands," he said, looking at me.

All right, I thought. Don't always shy away.

We sat down and I forgot how the slow opening, so sweet, and clear and delicate, made one reverential of life.

"Very nice," Lucia said, when we finished the first one.

Now we played in tandem, Sir Leo and me, and I was shockingly keeping in time. When I fumbled, I caught up to him and we were actually making music. Sir Leo added in the high notes, the ones that make your ribs ache, as you imagine a playroom with so much goodness of heart that that is what makes the crib rock.

"Empress of the Pagodas," he said, which is difficult, but he played the difficult parts and it was something. How could Lucia not love this man?

I had no time to think of anything else.

Now Conversations of Beauty and the Beast. I paid full attention to the notes, but what a brilliant idea, I thought. Was it Grimm who came up with that?

We all feel we're both Beauty and the Beast in love. I had forgotten how to be Beauty but now realized it was so much more relaxing than being the Beast.

On we played to the very beautiful ending, Sir Leo giving it all his beautiful sensitivity, the rising of the notes, with such assuredness, the crescendos up and down with the clock chime behind it and, when we finished, I was crying, as was Lucia, as was Sir Leo.

The oasis was inside here.

I got up, still tears in my eyes, and kissed Sir Leo and then kissed Lucia and left quietly, and walked down by the cypresses, still crying, so happy.

As I walked by the water, I thought, What are you so happy about?

And I got an answer that was so entirely new for me: You're not alone.

About the Author

Jacqueline Gay Walley has published eight novels; the most recent before *The Waw* is *Magnetism*. She has written plays (shown in New York and London) and has two films out based on her books. She has also written e-books such as *How to Write a First Novel* and other topics, which are available on Bookboon. Her film *The Erotic Fire of the Unattainable* was selected by six international film festivals and now plays on Amazon Prime. She currently lives in New York.

Books from Etruscan Press

Etruscan Press Is Proud of Support Received From

Wilkes University

Ohio Arts Council

The Stephen & Jeryl Oristaglio Foundation

Community of Literary Magazines and Presses

National Endowment for the Arts

Drs. Barbara Brothers & Gratia Murphy Endowment

Founded in 2001 with a generous grant from the Oristaglio Foundation, Etruscan Press is a nonprofit cooperative of poets and writers working to produce and promote books that nurture the dialogue among genres, achieve a distinctive voice, and reshape the literary and cultural histories of which we are a part.

etruscan press
www.etruscanpress.org
Etruscan Press books may be ordered from

Consortium Book Sales and Distribution
800.283.3572
www.cbsd.com

Etruscan Press is a 501(c)(3) nonprofit organization.
Contributions to Etruscan Press are tax deductible
as allowed under applicable law.
For more information, a prospectus,
or to order one of our titles,
contact us at books@etruscanpress.org.

Printed in the USA
CPSIA information can be obtained
at www.ICGtesting.com
JSHW081049140524
E13516000001B/1